ORPHEUS EMERGED

ALSO BY JACK KEROUAC

BOOKS
The Town and the City
The Scripture of the Golden Eternity
Some of the Dharma
Old Angel Midnight
Good Blonde and Others
Pull My Daisy
Trip Trap
Pic
The Portable Jack Kerouac
Selected Letters: 1940-1956
Selected Letters: 1957-1969
*Atop an Underwood: Early Stories
     and Other Writings*

POETRY
Mexico City Blues
Scattered Poems
Pomes All Sizes
Heaven and Other Poems
Book of Blues

THE DULUOZ LEGEND
Visions of Gerard
Doctor Sax
Maggie Cassidy
Vanity of Duluoz
On the Road
Visions of Cody
The Subterraneans
Tristessa
Lonesome Traveler
Desolation Angels
The Dharma Bums
Book of Dreams
Big Sur
Satori in Paris

ORPHEUS EMERGED

JOHN KEROUAC

INTRODUCTION BY ROBERT CREELY

ibooks
new york
www.ibooks.net

DISTRIBUTED BY PUBLISHERS GROUP WEST

ORPHEUS EMERGED

An Original Publication of ibooks, inc.

An ibooks, inc. Book

Distributed by Publishers Group West
1700 Fourth Street, Berkeley, CA 94710

ibooks, inc.
24 West 25th Street
New York, NY 10010

The ibooks World Wide Web Site Address is:
http://www.ibooks.net

ISBN 1-59687-123-7
First ibooks, inc. printing March 2002
First ibooks, inc. trade paperback printing, September 2005

10 9 8 7 6 5 4 3 2

Jacket design by Roger Gorman and Carrie Monaco
Interior design by Gilda Hannah

Printed in the U.S.A.

CONTENTS

FOREWORD

After Jack Kerouac died in 1969, his widow Stella kept his extensive archive private. Since her death in 1990, executor John Sampas has worked with publishers and scholars to bring Kerouac's unpublished work to light. Viking Penguin has published *The Portable Kerouac*, two volumes of *Selected Letters*, *Book of Blues*, *Some of the Dharma*, *Atop an Underwood: Early Stories and Other Writings*, and Joyce Johnson's correspondence with Kerouac, *Door Wide Open: A Beat Love Affair in Letters 1957-58*.

The allegorical novella *Orpheus Emerged* was completed in 1945, when the 23-year-old writer still signed his work "John Kerouac" and was deeply immersed in the process of finding the voice that came to express the spirit of a generation.

Kerouac wrote the novella shortly after meeting Allen Ginsberg, William Burroughs, Lucien Carr, and others in and around Columbia University. These friends would form the core of the group of writers known as the Beats, and they are reflected in the characters in *Orpheus Emerged*, a book filled with references to the books Kerouac was reading, the music and art he was discovering, and the concepts he was exploring.

Set in and around an urban university, *Orpheus Emerged* follows the obsessions, passions, conflicts and dreams of a group of colorful, searching, bohemian intellectuals and libertines. At its core is a *petit roman a clef*, a portrait of an artist as a young man torn between art and life—formulating his ideas about love, work, art, suffering, and ecstasy.

THINKING OF JACK

INTRODUCTION BY
Robert Creeley

IT WAS ALLEN GINSBERG who introduced us—if that's the appropriate word for what happened that evening in spring, San Francisco, 1956. I'd come into the city for the first time a few weeks before and had met Allen through the fact that both he and poet friend Ed Dorn were working at the Greyhound Bus Station on Market Street. So Allen had come up to the Dorns' apartment where I was staying— *crashed* is the better term—and we talked most of the night, remaining till Ed's shift was done. Not very long after Allen told us that Jack Kerouac's ship would shortly be coming into port in San Francisco and that if we went the next night to The Place, a local bar in North Beach run by old Black Mountaineers, he'd be meeting Jack there after work. At that time just one of Jack's novels had been published, *The Town and the City*, and that book by itself would probably have made little difference finally, either to us or the world. It was what hadn't been published yet—the great unwinding string of narratives, the veritable river of "spontaneous prose"—we so respected. Few had read any of it but the word was out. He was the astounding writer who had managed to keep a thousand pages moving wherein the only external action was a neon light going off and on out the window, over a drugstore across the street. So we went, hoping to meet the young novelist, already legendary at least to such as ourselves.

Memory recalls a young man sitting by himself at a far corner of the small space of the bar, just to the left of the turn for the toilets, where the sidewall met the back. There was no remarkable lighting focussed on him, but I do see him now as singular, isolated, quite still as he drinks. At some point he must have caught me looking at him, so he looks back—his eyes a striking blue, intense, very particular. I had no idea as yet this person was Jack but when Allen came in, seeing us, he asked if Jack had come, then saw the same fellow and said, "There he is!" Going over, we found his seeming quiet was a fact of his being altogether drunk, and I never did meet him that evening more than to help with getting him across the Bay and into bed in Berkeley.

I knew that drinking, however. I'd grown up in a farm town in New England close to Lowell, Jack's family home, some fifteen miles east. For us Lowell was the big city, along with places like Waltham. Boston itself was a glowing metropolis almost beyond imagination. My mother got my annual outfit for Easter in the Bon Marche in Lowell. Route 3 went through it on its way north to New Hampshire and the Boston and Maine Railroad took the same route as well along the Merrimac River. In the awkwardness of that time, drinking, it appeared, eased the male confusion, made inarticulate feelings far simpler to accommodate, and let one feel an unaccustomed comfort in the increasingly blurred surroundings. Whatever the fact, drinking was the way through, be it sexual delight—although how drunkenness helps such circumstance is hard to fathom—or rapport with a various social world not one's own. *Hale fellow, well met!* might quickly turn to *Throw that bum out!*—but by then one heard nothing anyhow.

So, in this poignantly fledgling novella what males do, along with write and talk, is *drink*—with women then as an ambience, even a resource and company, but always with a marked distance, made into objects as they are, from the real exchange apparent. If they do enter the action, it's with a wry and dislocating sense of contest. For example, Marie is Anthony's securing wife but then Anthony is given a determinedly vulnerable persona. When Marie goes off with Michael to have an "affair," she is the most substantial of all three. She also smokes!

> Michael followed her into the bedroom. Anthony was peacefully asleep, with just the hint of a smile on his lips.
>
> "What a big baby!" Michael exclaimed softly. Marie turned to him and almost smiled. But solemnly she said, "And what do you think you are?"
>
> "I'm not a baby."
>
> "Hmm?"
>
> Marie lowered the window pane, arranged Anthony's blankets, motioned Michael out of the room, and quietly closed the door. She went over to a desk drawer and took out a cigarette and lit it.

Jack's journals provide an interesting reference to *Orpheus Emerged*—"The Half Jest" as he calls it then—dated "Jan. 1944." As *The Book of Symbols* otherwise makes clear, he is casting his thoughts and work into large, symbolizing patterns with the sense of heroic forbears writ large indeed:

"Saroyan period," "Joycean period," "Wolfean period," "Nietzschean period (Neo-Rimbaudian)," "post-Nietzschean period (Yeats period)," which is where he locates *Orpheus Emerged*, "Spenglerian period," "American period (Dos Passos)," with the concluding one being the "post-neurotic period," aptly enough. It does him no disservice, like they say, to note that he is still not twenty-two years old. (His birthday is March 12, 1922.) No one's told him how to write other than what he's got from books as best he can. There's no defining tradition for such as he is, no social habit sustaining him. He's gloriously making it up as he goes along but trying with such moving determination to be a real writer, an encompassing writer, a great writer. When his lifelong friend and elder, William Burroughs, was asked to give his sense of Kerouac, he emphasized that, first and last, he was a *writer*.

Here then he is at work, at the beginning of it all, and whatever one makes of the result, it's fascinating to see his moves, call them, the interaction he manages between his characters, foretelling what will be the "story" of so much of his subsequent work. Allen Ginsberg is the character "Leo," for example, or so he seems to me. Who else would ask those charming questions? But it is the way the imagination of a life is conceived, that life and art must find a viable company, that the relations of men among themselves and with that outer "other" of women must be endlessly rehearsed—all such matters are those of his own life as book after book records.

"Art is the only true twin life has," Charles Olson, fellow poet, wrote in these same years. He lived in Gloucester and was said to be the inventor of "Projective Verse," just as Jack was credited with "Spontaneous Prose." In fact, there was even an edge of contest between the two groups comprising their followers as to just who was first in authority. Despite Olson's having written him in September 1957 to acknowledge his powers as a poet, Jack was not to meet Olson until well along in his life after he had come back to live in Lowell—as Olson had himself returned to Gloucester, to live on the upper floor of a fisherman's family house. One Sunday two of Jack's wife Stella Sampas' brothers drove him the short distance from Lowell to Gloucester to meet Olson. They sat in the car while Jack went in. As it happened, the *Boston Globe* had reviewed a novel of Jack's that day—which one I can't now remember—and gave it solid approval. Olson had taken the pages of the paper and spread them on the wooden steps outside leading up to his place, so that Jack might walk up in regal manner.

In America one has to find one's own way, step by difficult step. At any time there is much to be learned, much to be discarded, much to be engaged and contested. To the young man or woman it must seem often that the world they try finally to enter, whatever their hopes, has locked its doors. Is this what it means to be taught? To be nurtured? To be recognized as existing? Why doesn't Kerouac use the French he knows instead of those literary "Parisian" tags? Because he's learning, because he's young, because he wants to be let in. We know, of course, that a few years later it will be Kerouac who, as Allen Ginsberg usefully noted, makes the very transforming point, *that one can write in the same manner as one would speak to friends.* But now he is in New York, has dropped out of Columbia, is trying with all his powers simply *to write.*

There will never be another moment like this one.

—Buffalo, N.Y.
October 28, 2000

PAUL STOOD IN THE Book Shop facing a shelf of books. He came in every day at the same time, shuffling in his old shoes, and pored through the same score or so of books with his dirty fingers. And despite the complete disreputability of his appearance—the shabby clothing, the matted locks of dark hair protruding over the collar—and his constant smoking that filled the bright little Shop with smoke and its clean floors with cigarette ends, no one seemed to pay any attention to him. His daily visits had by now assumed the character of routine.

One or two of the clerks, however, were wont to comment on his habit of looking at the same twenty or so books every day. Nietzsche's complete works, a novel by Stendhal, Dostoyevsky's *The Idiot*, *Ulysses*, *The Oxford Book of English Verse*, and many others of this kind, he peered at impatiently each and every day, and always walked away from them with a preoccupied frown on his face.

It was a beautiful day in early Spring . . . Spring Day Eve, for a fact—when Paul was interrupted in his perusal of Kenneth Patchen's *Journal of Albion Moonlight* by Leo, a student at the University. Slim, dark haired, wearing blue horn-rimmed glasses, the boyishly ugly Leo hurried across the Shop and slapped Paul on the back.

"Paul!" he cried. "I heard you had been fired from your job. Is that true?"

Paul, glancing up to see who it was, and annoyed by the question, returned his attention to the book.

"You have!" ejaculated Leo, leaning toward Paul anxiously.

The other waved his hand and sent Leo stepping back. "Don't annoy me," he hissed sharply. "It's my affair. Don't start asking for details. Please shut up."

At this, Leo began to smile sporadically, and he bowed from the waist as a sign of deference. He could always manage to conceal his feelings.

"Where's Arthur?" Paul then inquired curtly.

"In class. I'm headed there now."

"I'll come," Paul said, and replaced the book on the shelf. He gave the shelf a last frowning look and started out to the street. Leo, at his heels, shrugged his shoulder doubtfully.

"You know, don't you," he said, "that the Professor is beginning to dislike your sitting in on his class. After all, you're not an enrolled student here . . ."

"I know, I know. He can do no more than throw me out of the class."

"Well that's true."

"Then come." Paul led Leo hastily across the street onto the green grass of the campus. He began to talk all at once. "Those books! If only I had time to read them, and more. This morning, after I lost my job, I went to the University Library itself, and do you know, there were hundreds of thousands of books there I honestly felt I should read! And the ideas that rush through my mind. The impatience I feel! The time running off like sand. Ah . . ." and he dismissed the question with a wave of his hand.

Leo laughed. "Do you know," he said, "this is about the fifth time you've told me that. Always, you're talking about books, and all the things to be learned, like Faustus in reverse himself. Arise, Paul! Come across the moonlit fields and seek the Golden Tree of Knowledge."

Paul almost sneered. He was hurrying along with his hands in his pockets. Despite his haste, he looked like a loafer of some sort, for his clothes were those of a tramp, and his shoe soles flapped rhythmically as he walked; and his large red and raw hands, like those of a peasant, were always in his pockets, so that he gave the conventional impression of the loafer and ne'er-do-well. Yet, he no longer created a sensation on the campus.

He had arrived two months ago, in February, "from the road," and from the North—and had taken a room on the campus, a sort of semi-coal-bin in the cellar of an apartment house on M street. He had immediately struck up an acquaintanceship with several of the students who had attracted his fancy in order to be accompanied to the use of the various cultural conveniences around the campus, such as the library, the music library, the art studio, and to be afforded a chance to sit in on lectures when he had occasion to. It was all very mysterious indeed. Some contended that he was a mere country bumpkin, come to the big city and the big university, without sufficient funds to register as a student. But others saw in him a great deal of sophistication and previous education, and dismissed the whole matter as some sort of psychopathic technique on his part.

Of Paul, Arthur had this to say one day to Michael, who lived on the campus with his mistress and was himself some sort of loafer: "Paul has something in his past that drives him like a madman. He is daemonic man personified! I wonder what it is?"

And to this, the laconic Michael only answered, "Yes, I suppose so. It must interest you a great deal. But as for me, I can't stand him." "It's because he's so much like you," Arthur had been quick to remark.

"*Peut-etre,*" Michael had replied, smiling faintly, and turning to resume the meal that had been set up on his work desk by his mistress, Maureen.

Now Leo led Paul into the classroom as he had done several times before in the past two months. The other students paid no notice, for none of them knew that Paul was not a registered student, except Arthur, who now rose to come greet the two young men.

"Paul," he said. "I hope it will go off today as it did last week, although I think our distinguished Professor is beginning to spout at the seams. Today's lecture, in case you're interested, will deal with the Zarathustra of Nietzsche."

"It's strange that he hasn't thrown you out yet," Leo put in. They took their seats in the last row of the class. "Perhaps he's discreet."

"Do you have any definite ideas on today's lecture?" Paul inquired of Arthur.

"Yes! You'll hear me air them in full. I have my notes here."

"And you'll manage as usual to get his gander up," Leo laughed.

"I, for my part, haven't had time to formulate anything specific," Paul said gloomily. He began to clean his fingernails with the nails of his other hand. "And of course, if I had, it wouldn't be right to speak up. I must keep my silence and listen. There's a limit . . ."

"Last night, at his apartment. He was writing a poem and wouldn't allow me to see it. He hardly acknowledged my presence!" Paul smiled craftily. "But of course, that can be expected of him. He's afraid of me."

"Have you known each other before?" Leo demanded.

"Oh yes."

"But Michael claims otherwise!"

"Well?" Paul smiled angelically, and almost began to blush. "That can be expected of him."

"I don't understand—" Leo began, but at this point, the Professor, bushy of eyebrow, had entered the class bearing a briefcase under his arm. From his mouth protruded a cigarette holder into which he had not as yet inserted a cigarette. Now he paused at the desk in front of the class and dramatically inserted a cigarette and lit it with a flagrantly large and decorative lighter.

"Gentleman," he said, and his eye fell on the disheveled Paul in the back of the room. "Good morning," he now concluded, addressing Paul directly. The latter blandly nodded back.

"Today's lecture," went on the Professor, talking straight at Paul with a great deal of irony in his tone, "deals with Nietzsche's great philosophical poem, 'Thus Spake Zarathustra.' "

The door of the classroom opened and a professor's head appeared, beckoning to the other. "William, a moment."

While the Professor was thus engaged outside, in the hall, Leo turned excitedly to Paul. "Now, tell me! You say that you knew Michael before? Where? When?"

"Some time ago. He refuses to admit it, of course."

"But why?" cried Leo in perfect agony.

Paul smiled. "It's all very involved and mysterious. I knew him when he was not the man he is today."

"Well tell us!"

"I shall, some time. You'll find out anyway"

The Professor had returned and now he sat on the edge

of the desk at the front of the class and began puffing meditatively on his cigarette.

" 'I bid you lose me,'" he began without warning, "'and find yourselves. Only when ye have rejected me, may I return unto you.' Does anyone recall reading these lines during the execution of the assignment?" There was more irony in this last remark, and the bushy eyebrows contracted portentously.

Arthur, glancing quickly over his class notes, now raised his hand.

"Well!" cried the Professor. "Do *you* remember it? Do you?"

"I remember it vaguely."

"Vaguely!" shouted the Professor with savage triumph. "And what does it mean to you?"

Arthur smiled mockingly at the Professor.

"Shall I be frank?"

"Frank?" The Professor puffed on his cigarette. "Yes, do!"

"Well—Zarathustra is speaking as the voice of ultimate society, and as society in general. I bid you lose me—society as it is, this pre-ultimate society—and find yourselves; and only when ye have all rejected me, this false, pre-ultimate society, this compromising civilization, may ye at last find Zarathustra, the ultimate, artistic society."

"Your own interpretation, I presume?"

"Precisely," answered Arthur quickly. Paul, who sat next to him, had begun to frown almost angrily.

The Professor was pacing in front of the class. "Do you think," he roared, "that Nietzsche can be embodied in your private desires? Heh?" Silence. "Is it ever going to be possible that anyone will resist reading himself into the man?"

The others of the class turned disconsolate faces on Arthur, as though he had been a culprit. Some of them were raising their hands tentatively in order to put in a word or two when Paul, who had by now reached a great state of suppressed excitement, jumped up on his feet and spoke:

"I thoroughly agree with you, Professor, where you condemn Arthur's liberal use of Nietzsche's meanings. But of course—that in itself is not the greater crime. Now, if you will permit me, I can point out where Arthur is making a far more serious mistake . . ." Paul paused here in order to catch his breath. The Professor was staring at him with something of indignation and outrage written on his face, but Paul ignored this.

"All asceticism," Paul began nervously, waving his large hands for emphasis, "is nonsense—and I construe Arthur's remark on the rejection of society as a broad, sweeping form of asceticism." Paul turned to Arthur, nodding his head at him eagerly.

"You see, now we are embarking on the business of

rejecting life, happiness, naturalness, for the sake of some dim ideal as the ultimate state or whatever it was. This is the first step towards the disease of good and evil, the first rather childish overture to false saintliness . . ."

Paul had lost all of his nervousness now, and the more he spoke, the more confident he became. He was just about to launch himself further into his little speech when the Professor held up his hand.

There was silence. But Arthur broke it by directly addressing his opponent: "What do you mean, false saintliness? Explain that, please . . ."

And Leo, sensing that all was not well, added eagerly: "Yes, do . . ."

But the Professor was not to be dissuaded. He was still holding up his hand, and the silence fell heavily all over. Some of the students had turned and were peering curiously at Paul, for they had grown accustomed to his silence on the occasion of his rare visits, and now, suddenly, he had burst out with a lot of nonsense that bewildered and annoyed them.

"Sir . . . whatever your name is, young man . . . you know, don't you," the Professor began, "the circumstances attending your presence here today, and several times previously in the course. I haven't mentioned it before, for reasons, er, commensurate with the unpleasantness involved."

Paul nodded and walked towards the door.

"I have a definite course to pursue in these lectures," the Professor went on, going to the door and blocking Paul's way, "and much of my time is very precious. Any interruptions. . . . Well, and there's the matter of my responsibility. If the Dean were to know . . ."

The Professor was opening the door. Paul quite suddenly bowed and smiled angelically to the Professor.

"Thank you, sir," he said. "I hope to meet you under more favorable circumstances in the future . . ." And with this he was gone, with the Professor looking after him with a rather preoccupied expression. Leo and Arthur, meanwhile, were exchanging anxious looks; but after the Professor had closed the door, and returned to his station at the front of the class as though nothing had happened, they rested easily.

After the hour, they found Paul waiting for them downstairs in the lobby of the building.

"Well," Leo called, "that's that!"

"Yes," said Paul, "it was good while it lasted." And with this, all three burst out into laughter and went out on the walk. It was lunch hour.

"You're going to have to do a lot of explaining to me about that false saintliness business," Arthur admonished in mock anger. "And Good Lord! What a mess you made of things, all because of your opposition to my ideas!"

"Where to?" Leo asked.

"Come with me," Paul said, hurrying off, "and we'll go to my room. You two must buy some sandwiches and we'll have lunch there."

"Again! Are you broke again?"

"Yes."

"He lost his job today," Leo explained to Arthur. "Tell us, Paul . . . What happened? Did you just walk out?"

"No, nothing like that. I stayed up late two nights ago trying to read all of Lucretius, *On the Nature of Things*, you know—and in the morning I couldn't get up. So when I reported for work today, poof! I was fired. There was another man running the elevator."

They were walking on M street. Halfway towards the boulevard, Paul turned in at an iron gate and led the two others down a short flight of stone steps to an iron grill-work door beneath the landing of the second floor entrance to the building. A narrow, dusty hall led to a crude, wooden door that opened with a loud scrape against the concrete basement floor.

Sitting on Paul's sagging cot was a gray-haired man of indeterminate age—he could have been anywhere from twenty-five to forty years old—who jumped up immediately and greeted Paul.

"Well, it's Anthony!"

"Paul!" repeated Anthony nervously, glancing at Leo and Arthur, who were depositing their books on the little table in the corner. "I came to see you about . . . Well, it's . . ." and Anthony could only look rather rudely in the direction of the two students.

Paul, sensing what was up, immediately handled the situation. "Go out and get the sandwiches, Leo, and you too, Arthur. Get me some beer to drink with it. We'll have another of our provocative luncheons."

"Yes," mocked Arthur, "in these, your luxurious chambers. All right, we'll be back in a minute." And with this, Leo and Arthur went out.

Anthony was instantly back on the couch with his hands over his face. Paul went over and sat at the table, and pretended to be absorbed in the examining of the tall oil lamp.

"I hit her!" Anthony announced, on the point of sobbing. "This morning. I've been looking for you since. I'm dying of . . . I can't face it!"

Paul smiled. "All right, all right. Let's get to the point of this."

Anthony had begun to weep.

"None of that," snapped Paul. "Till you've told me the details."

"Will you help me?"

"Of course, if I can."

"Oh," cried Anthony, starting to sob again, "my brother, my brother!"

"To the point!"

"Well—" and Anthony rose to walk back and forth across the little room.

"I struck Marie this morning; it was a stupid little argument over little things, but she had gotten the best of me, and I was suddenly enraged at her. Why? Can I tell you why? Can anyone explain why a man should suddenly strike his wife? By all let this be known, you know . . . the brave man—killing the one you love—with sword or kiss—in Oscar Wilde . . ."

"Go on!" cried Paul impatiently.

"Well—and I was a little drunk—"

"Is that all?" Paul shouted. "Then there's no problem. Go back to her this very minute and kiss her hand and weep there, not here . . ."

"I can't do it!"

Paul came over to Anthony and smiled at him. "Nonsense. You can. And Marie is accustomed to that sort of thing, anyway—she told me so herself. You struck her, you remember, about a month ago, when I first met you. Did Marie hold it against you? Did . . . But this is all a waste of time. Now, Tony, go immediately to Marie and do as I say. And don't be a baby!"

Anthony's lip was quivering.

"You're in a terribly nervous state," Paul added. "Otherwise you would realize how simple the whole thing is. Are you going now?"

Anthony hesitated. Then he started towards the door, shuffling his feet pathetically as though wishing to arouse his friend's sympathy. "Yes," he said, "I am."

"Goodbye. I'll see you tonight."

Anthony turned. "And we were supposed to go to the party tonight, now everything is terrible!—" He was almost on the verge of crying again.

"You'll make up, and you'll be at the party tonight. Goodbye! I'll see you when you're not in one of your neurotic moods, then we can have a talk about things, and enjoy a few drinks together."

Anthony began to chuckle. "I guess you're right. I'll go now. And without the fortitude of a drink, too. Watch me."

"All right." There was a minute or two of brooding silence . . .

"*A la vue!*" Anthony now flung carelessly. Then he paused again: "But it's going to be so hard. You don't understand me, Paul, although you claim to. You're too young! I'm older than you are, and I'm more complex . . ."

Leo and Arthur were at the door, pushing it in. They had packages of food with them. Without a word, Anthony walked past them and out, giving a show of resoluteness and purpose. Arthur motioned his thumb after the departing Anthony and said to Paul, "He's in a strange state! What's the matter?"

"Nothing, as usual," Paul said. "Now, let's eat."

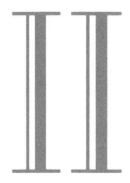

AS FAR AS MAUREEN WAS CONCERNED, Paul was by the way of being an unwelcome guest in her apartment—nay, an intruder. He was always neglected in his habits, and left cigarette butts around the house, sometimes in her flowerpots.

When Paul called at three o'clock that afternoon, Michael was out.

"Where is he?"

"He went out for a walk," answered Michael's mistress, disdaining to open the door any wider. "He's probably sitting in the park meditating or something."

"Well, then—" Paul reflected.

"No one is here," Maureen added unpleasantly. She was a woman in her late twenties, buxom, sensual—yet strangely maternal in her attitude towards the boy who lived with her. At times, however, her earthiness got the better of her maternal instinct, and she was wont to minimize the intellectualism of her lover.

Paul turned and started down the stairs. Then he paused and seemed to reflect again. "In the park," Maureen reminded him.

Paul turned his face up to her. "Don't worry, Maureen, I don't want to come into your house. I was just thinking."

"All of you are crazy," Maureen remarked sweepingly. She too had now begun to reflect. "All of you. I wonder sometimes what I'm doing here."

The boy grinned and went down a few more steps; then he stopped again. "Maureen," he said, "I won't come into your house if you don't want me to. I only come to see Michael, and if he's not in . . ." Maureen was silent. "So don't worry. I'm leaving now."

"Goodbye," said Maureen. "It's only that you dirty up the house."

"Yes," admitted Paul, "houses don't mean anything to me. If I had one, the wind would blow through it all year round and it would get all dusty and I'd freeze to death."

"All of you are crazy," Maureen repeated. "Back home, the kids aren't like all of you around here. They enjoy life, they have good times . . ."

"I'm looking for Michael," Paul put in. "You can tell me of your past the next time I come. I'm in a hurry now." Maureen slammed the door before he could finish, and so he descended the stairs and was presently out on the street. It was a warmish April afternoon, pregnant already with the sunny and lyrical thaw of an early spring.

Paul walked rapidly towards the park and scanned all the benches. He could not find Michael on any of them. Then he went back towards the campus, and crossed the street to go into the Boulevard Bar. Anthony was there, reeling in front of the counter and holding a glass of beer in his hand.

"This gentleman," Anthony announced as soon as he saw Paul, "has been kind enough to buy me drinks this afternoon. He is a sailor, a man of the sea." Paul nodded to the man who sat on a stool next to Anthony. "Reason? Because he has a social thirst, and craves to converse with a man well steeped, as I am, in Western culture."

"Largely Slavic," said the man, whose eyes seemed a trifle crossed, which gave him an appearance of zaniness. "Largely Slavic!" he repeated, for he too was drunk and repetitive. "Your friend, sir," he addressed Paul, "is a man of learning and manners."

Paul threw a coin on the counter and asked for a glass of beer.

"Your friend and I have been indulging in intellectual conversation this long afternoon," the man went on. "At sea, where there is but silence and ennui, a man develops a social thirst; and as soon as he reaches land, his first impulse is to venture forth to meet kindred spirits of his like, with whom to discuss and share the various beauties of wisdom."

Paul inwardly winced. He thought the man insane, for a moment, although he had a great deal of money with him. He had extracted a large bill from his wallet, and with a flourish, was ordering two more drinks for himself and his friend Anthony.

"Anthony," Paul said. "Have you gone to her today?"

Anthony did not answer.

"Have you?" But Anthony still did not deign to answer.

"You bungler," Paul hissed. "But ah—that is you all over, that's poor Anthony himself!" he added gloomily.

Anthony had now turned, and he shouted loudly and emphatically into Paul's face, "No, I did not go to see her!"

"All right," Paul said, and drank down his beer. "I'll have to go and see her myself, although I should be doing something else."

"Are you?" Anthony breathed. "Are you, Paul?"—and suddenly he had begun to sob. The sea gentleman looked very confused at all this.

"Excuse it all," Paul told the stranger. "Buy Tony some more drinks. Sit him over there in the booth, sit with him and discuss the beauties of wisdom as you call them. I'll arrange everything. There's a private matter, you understand. Anthony's meeting you saved him the emotional stress of executing a most painful . . ."

"I believe," interrupted the man, holding up his hand with tense drama, "I believe I begin to comprehend the entire matter. I believe so. I see. This friend, Anthony, is full of sorrow, and you are his friend. Very well. I shall take care of him."

Paul went over to Anthony, who was still sobbing, and pulled on his ear. "Anthony, shut up. Sit with your friend. I'm going over to see her now and everything'll be all right."

Anthony now sobbed more loudly than ever, and, having put his hand on Paul's sleeve, he was clutching it desperately. "You're too good, Paul, too good. Your goodness will kill you."

"Likely!" scoffed Paul, his eyes gleaming.

"My brother, my brother," bawled Anthony, making no attempt to control himself.

Paul finished his beer and turned to the man. "Take care of him. I'm going there now."

"Anthony is a man of great learning," the stranger pronounced. "And I understand he is a musician of no inconsiderable talent. I shall be honored to pay him my friendly respects for the remainder of the afternoon, perhaps far into the watches of the night indeed! . . ."

"Yes," Paul said.

"So do not worry, young friend. Everything—" Here, the man hiccuped and then turned his crossed, aimless glance back to focus in Paul's general direction. "Everything is in firm hands." Paul was certain that this man was mad. "Everything will come safely to port. You have entrusted your friend well . . ."

Paul was out on the Boulevard and as he began to walk toward Marie's house, he caught sight of Michael emerging from a doorway across the street.

"Michael!" he called, starting across the street in a half-trot. But Michael, at the same instant, had caught sight of Paul, and he had begun to walk away very swiftly. Paul persisted in his chase, until Michael, turning to see that it was hopeless, decided to run—and run he did, so that in a few moments, he had disappeared around a corner and was gone.

Paul gave it up and stopped in his tracks. He shrugged his shoulders and muttered under his breath. "He will continue to be stupid like that. He insists on running away, as though it were in any way possible. It's all a waste of time, that's all I care! Time. He's having his so-called season in hell, ha-ha."

Paul walked for a while, thinking, until suddenly he realized that he had passed Marie's house. He turned and hurried back towards his original destination. Breathless—for all the hurrying—he arrived in the lobby of her apartment house and glanced at the brass plates near the buzzers. He rang her buzzer and was soon admitted. He went up the stairs, where Marie had already left open her door, though she herself was not standing in the doorway. "May I come in?" Paul shouted through the open door.

"Of course," answered a quiet voice, Marie's, from the front room.

Marie was wearing her rose-colored pajamas, seated on the bright quilt laid out on the divan, and smoking a red-tipped cigarette. The radio was on to a Bach organ fugue.

"And where is my darling?" Marie said straight off, with

mockery in her tone. "Did you close the door?"

"I just saw him. Yes, I closed the door. Marie—he is weeping."

Marie snuffed down her nose contemptuously. "Shut up about that weeping! Do you think that when a thing is a rule, and not an exception, it'll continue to move one? Ghastly!"

"Marie, you're cruel—but sensitive."

"Thank you."

"Marie, you must realize that Anthony is not a well man. He's a lot like I am now, you see, but of course, of course, he doesn't have what I have. He's searching, you see . . . I've my Helen, and—"

"Stop babbling," interrupted the girl.

"Do you realize," Paul went on unconcernedly, throwing himself on the divan next to Marie, "that love is painful, that it makes a man like Anthony suffer? Oh, I know, I know—it's all the pain of happiness. But he is the weeping kind. And do you realize, my dear, that if he is weak, he can do nothing about it? So he hit you this morning! . . . and for that little slap in the face, he's endured upon himself an eight-hour session of imponderable sorrow, unspeakable *angoisse*."

"You crazy child!"

"Does your face hurt? Does your face hurt?"

"Shut up."

"His heart is broken, Marie, you diabolical witch! . . ."

"You came here to call me names?"

"Yes, because I love you."

Marie got up from the couch and threw her cigarette out the open window. Then she stopped in front of the radio and laughed.

"Ha ha," mocked Paul, getting up also. "It's just that I love you enough to want you to love Anthony, and I know Anthony well . . ."

"My God!" cried Marie. "You're mad, aren't you?"

"No, no."

They were silent, and Paul began to pace the rooms.

"Now," he said at length. "I come to see you as Anthony's envoy, to tell you that he is weak, and that he's sorry, and that nothing matters but that you love him as he loves you. Can you do that? Can you do that?"

"Can I do that?" Marie echoed contemptuously. "Have you eaten lately?"

"Yes."

"I'll heat you some soup. You're in a delirium."

Marie went off into the kitchen, with Paul right at her heels, talking furiously. "Marie, will you forgive him? Oh, this waste of time!! People waste all their time. They're alive for just so long, and they waste their time on recriminations and retributions and all such nonsense. Wait, you'll find out all about me some day, and you'll realize what I'm saying. You might meet my Helen . . . Give me some soup, yes, and some bread. I am rather hungry . . ."

Marie was calmly giving him a piece of bread, and removing a soup bowl from the cupboard. The soup was heating on the stove.

"A lovely kitchen," Paul was saying. "Tell me, Marie. What shall I do? Shall I get Anthony, sober him up, and bring him here?"

"No. He's got to come of his own accord."

"Then my words have done some good?! . . . haven't they?"

"No, not your words. I love my husband. We'd have made up eventually. I dare say we don't need your help, either."

"Ha ha!" cried Paul. "I'm a time saver . . ."

"Balderdash!"

Paul sat at the little table and took the spoon Marie had offered him. "You see," he cried, "I've done some good. I've saved time. Accept Anthony, accept him . . . he's a good man, a wonderful soul. He's weeping in the Boulevard Bar now, because he struck you . . ."

"You nor anyone else can't patch up our troubles," Marie said, placing the steaming bowl of soup before the hungry Paul. "Anthony strikes me . . . it's his problem. No one else can help. That's why he weeps, you little fool, because he realizes that he alone is guilty."

"And you?"

"I, of course, have my share of guilt. And it's none of your business, little Jesus Christ. I'm restless and intolerant, and I never seem to have made up my mind one way or another about Anthony. Well . . ."

Paul slurped up several spoonfuls of soup and then jumped up. "Now I've got to go. I'm pressed for time, goodbye, and look I'll take this bread with me. Thank you . . ." And suddenly, Paul had walked out of the kitchen and was gone.

Marie picked up the bowl from the table and emptied the soup in the sink. She went to the door and closed it, for Paul had forgotten to close it in his haste. Then she went back to her divan and sat down with a freshly-lit cigarette. She was smiling secretly.

The buzzer rang again and she thought it was Paul rushing back to say something further. But a few moments later, Michael knocked at the door and walked in.

"It's you," Marie said.

"You coming to the party tonight?" Michael asked outright.

"Sit down," Marie said. "Yes, I suppose so. You must

remember that it's Maureen's party."

"I don't care. I want to see you."

"You and your inconvenient remarks," Marie said.

"Well? And who cares?" Michael had sat down in a chair in the other room and was watching Marie gloomily. There was a silence during which nothing further needed to be said.

"I've fixed up a little apartment in the Quarter," Michael finally said. "I expect you soon." His tone was firm, but gloomy.

Marie did not reply. She was watching him with something of weariness in her demeanor. Finally, she said: "What do you expect of me?"

"I only expect you to be sensible."

"What? You want me to leave my husband for a while! You call that sensible?"

"Of course. For both of us. I desire you, that's all there is."

"And suppose I didn't desire you, as you so romantically put it?"

"Why can't you?"

"I don't think you're capable of a decent affair, that's why I can't. You neurotics are all the same as lovers. Foo! Go home!"

Michael began to smile sardonically.

"How can you be so sure?" he asked. "I know, I know also by the expression on your face that the idea appeals to you. You know that I have money and that we can have the best for as long as we want it to last. You also need a change, I can sense that in your voice."

"Nonsense."

Michael got up, and, without a word, walked out of the apartment. He left Marie in a very pensive mood.

IN THAT LAND, the biggest holiday of the year occurs on the 27th of April, which is usually the first fine day of spring, and if not—the weather being unfavorable—it is at least a day breathing with the first sharply defined odor of spring, and rife with its gentleness.

Now, Maureen had planned a party for the eve of the Spring Day, and all that day—even during Paul's unwelcome visit—she'd been very busy preparing the apartment for the festivities. Michael had given her some money with which to buy things to prettify the rooms, and also for hors d'oeuvres and such things as are served at parties.

Maureen had taken great care in setting out flowers throughout the house, for she loved flowers, and candles, and brightly colored bowls full of nuts and candies.

It was seven o'clock before she allowed herself time to sit down and rest. By that time, Michael was back from his afternoon stroll, and was deeply absorbed in his writing. The invitations had been sent out, and their friends would start coming sometime around nine o'clock.

"And dinner?" Michael demanded, looking up from his desk. Maureen gave him a beseeching look. "It's out we go for dinner, then," Michael concluded. He was in good spirits now, and had just written some lines that met with his judged approval; and just the night before, he had completed a philosophical essay of which he was inordinately proud. "Come," he said now, "let's go down to a good restaurant—how about the Lobster Shack?—and have something delicious to eat. Lobster, steamed clams, anything you like."

They went to dinner and, as they were crossing the

campus, Leo accosted them. "Well, well—hello. And the big party tonight, I've got my invitation with me right here. I've just wound up my studies, and I was on my way over to your place now. Thought it wouldn't be out of place to come a little early."

"It would," Michael replied gruffly. "Maureen and I are going to eat. She's been preparing the apartment all day."

"Well, can I accompany you to the restaurant? I've nothing else to do. Although I've already eaten . . ."

Michael smiled shyly. "All right, Leo." Each time he was gruff to Leo, and each time that the other yielded so stickily, he became ashamed of himself. He was not a sadist, not Michael except where it gave him pleasure, and for that his attacks needed a contained resistance of a sort, such as Maureen offered him.

They had dinner while Leo drank coffee and babbled endlessly about his studies and about Paul. Maureen was in a pleasant mood, and she was enjoying her lobster thermidor and paying no attention to Leo. "Now," she said at length, "we'll go back, and I'll get things done for good. Oh, Michael darling," she said, while Leo was off to buy cigarettes at the counter of the restaurant, "say that you love me."

"Just for today? Spring Day eve?"

"No, for always." Maureen squeezed Michael's hand

beneath the table. She was ten years older than Michael, and each time that she squeezed his hand in a public place, it reminded Michael unpleasantly of his mother, and of the way that she too used to show affection in public places. "Are you happy?" she asked.

"Certainly. You're a fine woman, Maureen; and I love you very much."

"Say that you'll never go away from me."

"I'll never go away from you," Michael said. Sometimes, when they were in bed, she would make Michael repeat those words over and over again while she held his head in her bosom and rocked back and forth. Michael, by nature very non-committal, could always cope with these situations by the sheer weight of his general indifference toward life.

"I wish," went on Maureen wistfully, "that we could fall in love like those two, Anthony and that Marie."

"Do you think so?" Michael asked, frowning. "Look at poor Anthony . . ."

"I know, but it's that witch of his, Marie—even though I can't see what she sees in him, he's such a drunkard and a pest sometimes."

Leo was back. "Come on," he said, "let's go out while it's still light, and take a little walk."

They went out and strolled around the campus. Michael

had bought a cigar and was puffing it contentedly. He was already on fire with a new poem—he would go right straight to bed, now, and prop up on some pillows and write it.

It was just sundown when they had returned to X Street. A bird was sitting on the top branch of a small poplar in front of their apartment house entrance. Michael stopped and looked up at the bird.

Leo laughed. "Hail to thee, blithe spirit . . ."

"No," cried Michael, "quiet, Leo. Listen to him. Do you remember what I was telling you about the impulse of God? The sparrow there is expressing it. He knows. Listen!"

"My God," said Maureen. "Are we going to stand here for hours listening to the impulse of God?"

"Of course not," said Michael, with some annoyance. "I'm sleepy. I'm going to take a nap before the party begins. Listen to the sparrow. Its imagination is filled with God . . ."

They all three were silent as the bird trilled. Michael smiled secretly. He looked up at the street and saw, over the library roof, the last faint hues of the sunset. "The bird," he went on, "is singing the song of dusk, on Spring Day eve. Could there be more perfect happiness? Not just to be expressing, but to be your expression. Isn't that love? Isn't that life?" he now asked harshly of Leo. "Isn't that more than human love, than human life, more, much more?"

"Foo!" said Maureen. "Let's go up."

"What do you mean?" Leo asked, showing eager interest, and lighting up a cigarette.

Michael began, "I mean—" But Maureen had clutched at his arm.

"Look," she whispered. "There's that Paul."

Michael and Leo turned nervously in the direction she had indicated with her head. Paul was standing in the shadows of a doorway just a few feet away watching them. There was a brief silence, during which the bird too had interrupted its song.

"Well?" Maureen said warily.

"What are you doing there?" laughed Leo. "You're a ghost; you hover in doorways. Come here. Are you coming to the party tonight?"

Paul did not answer, nor did he move away from the doorway.

"Are you?"

"I wasn't invited," he said quietly and casually.

Michael turned to Maureen, but kept his tongue. Leo fell into an embarrassed silence.

"Of course," Paul went on quietly from his doorway, "of course, my not being invited has nothing to do with anything. You all know me well, and my ways. I may walk into the middle of the party, and no one will object. It's only Paul, they'll say, and he does things like that . . ."

"That's right," Michael interrupted in a surly tone. "So why do you have to bemoan that part of it."

Paul smiled and began to walk away up X street.

"Are you going to come anyway?" Michael suddenly called. This came as a great surprise to both Maureen and Leo, and to Paul himself no less. He stopped in his tracks and stood still, stiffly, as though a stunning thought had just shot into his mind. Maureen gave Michael a strange, puzzled look, and Leo was again vaguely embarrassed.

Paul had not yet turned, was still standing numbly, as though struck.

Michael strode up the steps and into the dark hall of the apartment house. Maureen followed, while Leo, for his part, wavered near the steps, to wait and see what Paul would do. Paul had not yet moved, not yet turned, and although Leo hesitated at least ten seconds while Michael and Maureen were going up the steps, he did not see Paul move, and reported it so later.

Michael immediately went to his bed to lie down, stating that he would sleep awhile and wake up in time for the party. Before he could fall asleep, Maureen questioned him about Paul. "I thought you didn't want him around. I felt sure you wouldn't have liked my inviting him to the party, he's such a madman, and a lot of people don't want him around."

"Who for instance?" Michael illogically pouted.

"Well, my friend Barbara."

"Barbara is a bore."

"She is not! And she's a nice girl, and a whole lot smarter than the lot of you with all your fancy talk."

"Oh shut up. I want to sleep now."

"Don't shut me up, you brat!" Maureen shouted, and she hit Michael with his own shoe that lay at the foot of the bed.

"Is this the way to start a party!?" called Leo from the other room, where he was satisfying his aesthetic impulse by moving the flowers around to different parts of the room. "Yelling at each other. Look, I've arranged things nicely here. Look at it."

"Now I'm sleeping," said Michael, and turned over.

"Yes, and you'll wrinkle your trousers. I just pressed them this morning."

Michael sighed, rose from his bed, removed his trousers, handed them to Maureen, and lay down again to sleep. "Close the door," he added.

"The dreamer, the dreamer," said Leo, with his face in the bedroom door. "Tell me what you dream this time, Michael. 'Life, you impalpable phantom, thrust not your fog shapes at me, I reject you! Oh dreams! Oh powerful, tangible dreams—I'll dream till death is a dream!' He wrote that himself, Maureen, now look at him. He's—"

"Shut up," interrupted Maureen. The doorbell was ringing. "Answer the bell," she ordered Leo. She closed the door and Michael was left to sleep.

"It's Arthur and Toni!" Leo cried from the hall. "And they have wine and record albums with them. Hello, hello, hello. And Julius is with them. Hello Julius. Come in, come in, the place is all fixed up; you won't recognize it! What's that you've got under your arm, Arthur? Ha! T. S. Eliot. 'Ash Wednesday,' is it?"

" 'Quartets,' " corrected Arthur, brushing into the room with his load of records. Maureen was standing arranging the candy bowls and preparing to light the candles.

"Well, well," cried Arthur, "how nice everything is! And Maureen—you look beautiful. Where's Michael?"

"Taking a nap."

"Taking a nap, taking a nap. Toni, see how nice these gladiolas are."

Toni entered the room demurely and smiled at Maureen. "My God," she said, looking around, "the place doesn't look the same. You must have been working all day. Is Barbara coming?"

"Yes."

"Yes, indeed," Julius echoed softly, and sat down on the couch. Leo sat down next to him and offered him a cigarette. "Julius," he said straight off, "what happened during your trip?"

"I rode," he answered. "I rode and I rode."

"Wine!" cried Arthur, holding up a bottle of vermouth. He held it up to the candlelight. "See the color? Get some glasses, somebody."

The doorbell rang again.

"Wait!" cried Leo, jumping up. "Everyone's coming early. It's going to be some night. That must be Anthony and Marie. Perhaps they have some wine too."

Julius had stretched out on the couch and was perusing a volume of Baudelaire's works. "Take your big feet off my couch," Maureen warned as she ran up to the kitchen to fetch glasses. Toni was standing in front of the mirror preening her hair.

Anthony and Marie came in, and soon the party was well underway.

"Big surprise!" cried Arthur, holding up his albums of records for all to see. "I have here the Brahms Clarinet Quintet in G minor. We're going to play this and also some others I have here. Stravinsky's Petruchka ballet suite, who likes that?"

"I do, I do!" cried Anthony happily.

"I borrowed these from Bartholomew, the capitalist aesthete. Look! And here I have Shostakovich's Fifth, the 'Apassionata Sonata' and shorter pieces."

"Shostakovich!" cried Anthony wildly, running up to Arthur. He had already begun drinking, and had a head start on everyone else. "Let me hold it to my heart! And here, you didn't show us this one . . . Rachmaninoff! His Second Concerto! Marie, Marie," he cried, turning to his beloved. "The Russian soul!"

"Yes," she said, "I know."

"Said the rooster to the hen, or something," Julius mumbled from the couch. "Is this the Slavic soul I've heard so much about?"

"What is it from?" cried Leo, reflecting. "I read it somewhere . . ."

The doorbell was ringing again.

"Barbara that must be, and her friend Hubert!" Leo went on, hurrying towards the hall. "I'll bet it's them. That completes it, all right . . ."

"Only the Russians know how to write music," Anthony was saying to Julius, who lay demurely on the couch. "Don't talk to me about those damned classic forms. Pah!

Rachmaninoff!" he shouted, carried away again with excitement. "Rachmaninoff!" Anthony had not yet taken his hat off, he was too excited; it was a slouch hat, dark and limp, and he looked utterly fantastic in it. "Let me hold it to my heart!!" he repeated, picking up the album.

Barbara, a girl about Maureen's age, and her escort, Hubert, were the last to arrive. Immediately after, with the serving of wine and hors d'oeuvres, and the beginning of the record concert, the party was in full swing—and Michael still slept.

Anthony had insisted on beginning the concert with Stravinsky's Petruchka suite, but Arthur protested, and they compromised on playing excerpts. All during the performance, Anthony was in raptures; and he would have started dancing hadn't there been so many people, or, rather, hadn't he had so little wine as yet. When the music was finished, and everybody applauded, and the hubbub grew, Arthur and Anthony argued violently over the next piece to be played.

"But did you notice," Arthur put in, after they had come to an agreement, "that peculiar ebullient quality in Petruchka, in all of Stravinsky? Eh? I would compare that art with that of Tchelichev, and with Joyce too."

"Yes, yes," nodded Anthony, drinking up some wine. Julius was at their side. "You know why?" Arthur went on.

"Well, it should be evident. It seethes with life—there are great eruptions of organic matter, and behind a sort of ripple of amoebae. Ho! That's good!"

"Vaguely," said Julius. "Tell me, Arthur. Since I've been gone, I hear you've been espousing poetry. Can I lay that to Michael's influence?"

"Perhaps," said Arthur, putting the new record on the machine. "This!" he now cried to the party in general, "is the new Brahms Clarinet Quintet in G minor. Everybody listen!"

The music started, but this time everybody kept talking; wine had loosened all their tongues. They were assembled in little groups throughout both the rooms. Arthur sat rapturously by the machine, while Anthony sulked over by the couch. "Only the Russians know how to write music," he insisted darkly, but Arthur paid him no attention.

"Well, tell me," Julius persisted, sitting by Arthur. "Tell me now in all seriousness: What does the modern poet want, hey?"

"That's a vague question. But perhaps I can answer it. Yes! He wants a return to the conditions of the Golden Age."

Julius chuckled softly. "That does sound like Michael. You know, I know him better than you think. He's got you in his grip . . ."

"What are you talking about?"

"Oh, nothing. But—" and Julius chuckled again—"that business of wanting a return to the conditions of the Golden Age, you know that sounds terribly like the phrase, 'he wants a return to the conditions of the nursery,' now doesn't it?"

Arthur waved an impatient hand.

Just after the music ended on the phonograph—at the termination of the second movement of the quintet, to be exact—and as everyone began clapping their hands, and laughing and talking while Arthur somewhat proudly and bashfully removed the record from the turntable, Michael gloomily emerged from his bedroom.

There was a pause in the hubbub, and then Leo cried out his name and ran up to him with a glass and a bottle of wine: "Here, here, help yourself to some wine! Wake up! . . . you're half asleep."

Michael stared sullenly at Leo, rubbing his eyes with his knuckles. Then he gradually became conscious of the large group assembled in the two rooms, most of whom were staring and smiling at him, for he was technically and undeniably the "host."

"All right," smiled Michael bashfully, taking the bottle and the glass. "I guess I do need to wake up. I had only intended to take a nap . . ."

"Famous last words!" cried Julius, and at this time, the tension was released: laughter and babble were resumed, during which Michael, with a sort of sigh of relief, poured himself some wine and drank it. At this point, the doorbell rang once more, and Leo immediately dashed into the hall. Maureen, excitedly relating something to her friend Barbara in the next room, had not heard the ringing. Michael sat down on the couch and began to scratch his hair sleepily.

"Well, well, Mike," said Arthur, coming over. "You missed the Brahms quintet."

"On the contrary, no," Michael said, smiling up at Arthur. "It woke me up; I listened in bed. It was comfortable in bed and the music was soothing, particularly the second movement—although there was so much noise I could hardly hear it."

"It's wonderful music," said Arthur, sitting down beside Michael. He lit a cigarette.

Michael drained another glassful of wine. He smacked his lips. "Can you imagine that music?" he said eagerly. "Those slow movements? God! What an incredibly sensitive man Brahms must have been, to feel that type of thing in him . . ."

"It's Paul!" Leo cried from the hallway. "Come on in, friend. We have wine, music, everything. We've all been waiting for you, as you so accurately predicted . . ."

There was an answering mumble. Arthur rose from the

couch and went into the hallway. "Hi there, you . . ."

Michael picked up his bottle and glass and stood up irresolutely. Then he walked quickly to the other room and stood at the fringe of a group comprised of Anthony, Marie, Toni and Barbara's friend Hubert. They were talking about the latest psychological advances, and Hubert was holding forth on hypno-analysis. Michael refrained from looking directly at Marie; instead, he concentrated his gaze on Toni, Arthur's blonde girl, and would have spoken to her hadn't she been so engrossed in what Hubert was saying.

"It's a great thing," Hubert was saying, motioning with his long thin hands. "Certain blind spots deny you and the psychoanalyst both an insight into certain important matters. Under hypno-analysis, of course, one lets loose completely—the blind spot becomes and illumined eye . . ."

"You turn your phrases like a poet," Michael interrupted suddenly, and without warning to the little group. "Let me tell you," he rushed on, as the others stared at him with some surprise, "in psychoanalysis one very important factor is completely overlooked, as far as I am concerned, you see—although I'm no expert on the subject." Hubert was staring coldly. "So you're given an adult insight into child emotions which have formed certain emotional patterns in you, so that is so . . ."

"Well," began Hubert. Michael held up his hand. At this instant, Anthony caught sight of Paul in the next room and shouted at him across the apartment. "Paul, Paul, you've come. It worked, you know!" And with this, Anthony ran to Paul, and as he disengaged himself from the little circle of conversation, he left a little place for Michael to step into. Before the others could turn their attentions to the effusive greeting Anthony was tendering Paul in the next room, Michael rushed on, hardly knowing what he was talking about: "You see, now, as I was saying, look! The analysis regains your right, psychologically speaking, to make adult decisions. It has revealed to you certain blind spots, say as hypno-analysis does, it is a revelation. What can I find out about myself, for instance, hey? Plenty, plenty. But I refuse to find out!—it would ruin me, I would no longer contain dark secrets, and nightmares, and dualisms, and thrilling conflicts. No, I would be left completely cleaned out of all my poetic equipment, and I would have to say, in a broad sweeping voice, 'Now—I begin anew!' and the world would ask, well he has cleared out all the decks, well? So now, what does he have to say? That's what I mean by what I was saying! Don't you see the psychoanalysis rids you of the rich store of your imagination, it thieves you, rich thievery, ha ha!"

Hubert, strangely enough, seemed to be interested in all

this prattle, despite its incoherence, and was maintaining a polite attitude of receptivity; but of Marie and Toni, this could not be said. Subtly, they had opened a sub-discourse of their own and were now standing slightly apart from the two men, and any moment they would find the opportunity to casually walk away. Meanwhile, in the other room, there was great noise, with Paul at the center of it all. He had come in wearing a rose in his hair, and everybody seemed to be deriving great enjoyment out of this. Paul was now taking the flower out of his hair—he had previously purchased it in the flower store on M Street—and with a deep bow and a flourish, he was presenting it to Maureen.

"To the hostess, charming and lovely," he said. "A rose to keep you when you're sad. Food for the stomach, love for the heart, a rose for melancholia." He made a dramatic gesture as she took the rose from his hand. It was evident that he had been drinking, for as he straightened up from his bow, he tottered and wavered.

"You know don't you," Hubert was now telling Michael, who had turned his eyes to the slightly maudlin scene in the other room while Hubert was seriously absorbed in their topic, "that what you're saying is, to me, a whole mess of theoretical and aimless nonsense?"

"Yes?" Michael said politely. "By the way, have we met before?"

"No. My name is Hubert. How do you do." They shook hands. Hubert went on: "What did you precisely mean?"

"Another thing," Michael said, "before I explain the latter: it might as a matter of fact illumine my whole conception of psychology as a whole. Now. Do you know, for instance, why my output—I am a writer, I write poetry and other things—why this output is so large, why I keep steadily writing? It's because of what you would call an insecurity sense in psychology. Now, look, suppose I were to rid myself of this insecurity sense through psychoanalysis, I would not be driven to my work as before a wind—perhaps I would never write again, because I'd find out what it is that makes me want to write, to create . . . !"

Hubert digested this slowly and with a serious mien. Then he took a sharp little intake of breath. "Overlooking the assumption," he said slowly, with precision, "that . . . creation . . . might not necessarily be your supreme individual function, why should quantity of output be set up as an argument against psychoanalytical house-cleaning?"

This quite overwhelmed Michael; and on top of that, he wasn't listening very attentively. He was annoyed that Marie and Toni had wandered away from his conversation. He merely nodded, his eyes on Marie, who stood in the other room talking to Julius, radiant in red slacks, with a red ribbon in her dark hair, and a sort of crimson shell bracelet on her slender wrist. Michael, half-awake, feverish from wine and sleepiness, could not take his eyes off her.

Hubert, with his eyes fastened on Michael's face, was going to say something else devastating when Barbara suddenly ran up to him and pulled him into the next room to show him the watercolor reproduction of Degas' "Interior" over the small table in the corner. There was complete chaos everywhere in the apartment, as is to be expected at a gathering where wine has begun to be the moving spirit. Michael was left standing alone, and he began to sulk. He went to the window and looked at the night outside in an attempt to seem composed. The noise behind him was beginning to annoy his nerves.

Leo came up and handed him a glass of wine. "Come on, you're way behind everybody. Drink up! What's the matter with you, you seem annoyed?" The first notes of Shostakovich's Fifth Symphony rang out behind them.

"Too much noise," Michael mumbled. He drank the wine. "And I've been snubbed," he added sharply.

"What?" Leo laughed. But Paul was suddenly beside them, laughing also.

"Snubbed, Michael?" he said, slapping the latter on the back. "You resent it, my asocial friend? How were you snubbed? Who? Ha ha ha."

Michael turned a glowering countenance on Paul.

"You don't like people," Paul mocked. "You hate people. Your emotions are unreservedly aesthetic, aren't they? Didn't you tell me that when you left? . . ."

"When he left where?" Leo asked curiously. "What's all the mystery?"

"Shut up," said Michael to Leo. Suddenly, Paul was standing just in front of Michael, and swaying a little.

"I need some money," he said quietly. "I just spent my last sous on a few drinks and a flower for Maureen."

"Well?" Michael grunted, turning away.

"I've lost my job. I can't work. I'm too nervous. Michael, I've had enough of this anyway. If you can't . . . well, at least give me some money. I'm hungry, damn you!"

Leo began to edge away in embarrassment, but he couldn't bear to miss what was going on, so he hovered a few feet away and pretended to be absorbed in his glass.

Michael was morosely silent. Paul waited. Then finally Michael withdrew several bills from his wallet and pushed them to Paul across the top of the bookcase that stood beside them. Leo could not help noticing that it was an unusually large sum in view of the circumstances.

Paul put the money in his pocket and said, "Thank you." Michael gave him a look drenched with contempt, put out his hand to push Paul out of the way, and strode into the other room to mingle with the others.

Paul turned to Leo and smiled happily. "Come on, Leo," he said. "Let's have some more wine. This is a wonderful party."

"I should say it is," Leo drawled significantly. Paul's eye flashed for just a moment, but then he began to laugh heartily at Leo's hint and dragged him along into the other room, to the table where the bottles were. They poured themselves some wine.

"Leo," said Paul, "I've a little *acte gratuit* in mind. Did you ever hear of the *acte gratuit*—as in Gide, for instance? I was reading him the other week. People commit atrocities on an impulse, but the impulse is gratuitous, there's no reason for it."

"I know," said Leo. "What about it?"

"I have here a little *acte* that is not entirely gratuitous. But just because it's so coldly premeditated, it becomes more than an *acte gratuit*."

"What on earth are you driving at?"

Smiling, Paul raised his glass and poured some wine down the back of Leo's collar. Leo yelled excitedly and backed away. "What's that? What's that for?" But Paul, laughing loudly, was patting Leo on the back.

No one had noticed this little incident, except for Julius, who lay languidly on the couch watching every move that Paul made. He had been the only one in the party, as well, who had seen the exchange of money between Michael and Paul.

"You're crazy!" Leo spluttered at Paul, wiping his neck with a handkerchief, half-angry, half on the point of laughing good-naturedly. He couldn't quite express what he really felt about Paul's having poured wine on him. "You're a sadist, I think, Paul."

"Just a little premeditated *acte gratuit*," Paul said. "I took great pains to explain everything . . ."

Julius had sauntered over to them.

"A little wine bath for little Leo?" he inquired softly. "Paul, you do surprise me sometimes. What a strange form of revenge!"

"Revenge!" mocked Paul. "I don't know what you mean . . . revenge." But Julius maintained a teasing silence.

"Julius," Paul said at length, "I think you'd better get back to your couch and observe further events—for you are an observer, you know, you observe things, that's why you live. A super-*voyeur*. But your fault is that you think yourself omniscient. You types are all the same; you think you have everything figured out. Now," said Paul, taking a letter from a pocket of his filthy jacket, and waving it at Julius, "try to figure this out." He started away, then he came back and looked closely at Julius. "Ah, now I see. You saw Michael giving me money. Tell me, omniscient one, what was that for? Explain it."

"Perhaps I'm not up to it," Julius said.

A clamorous Shostakovich sequence thundered behind them, with Anthony's happy yells exceeding all other sounds.

"Come now," said Paul. "Do you suspect that Michael is my brother?"

"I'm not saying a word," Julius smiled.

"And that I punished Leo for thinking cheaply of the money incident, hey?" Julius still smiled. "All figured out?" Paul cried. "Then watch this—oh, by the way, this will mark the end of the party!" And, saying this, Paul started off again with the letter in his hand, going straight to Michael, who was standing with Arthur listening to the latter's anecdote of his last foray into the Bohemian Quarter.

Paul thrust himself between them, waved a letter before Michael's face, and said: "Michael, I have a letter."

Michael frowned and pushed the letter away. "All right, so you have a letter. What do I care?"

Paul smiled. "But it's from Helen."

Michael opened his mouth in an expression of great exasperation; but suddenly, as he understood Paul's words, the expression turned to that of pain—pain and anguish. He seemed on the verge of a stroke, he had become so pale and trembling, with his fists knotted hard at his sides.

"And she's coming here soon," Paul added, still waving the letter.

Michael seemed to take a deep breath, with his lips compressed; then suddenly he emitted a loud yell of rage at Paul and pushed blindly at him. Paul backed up a few steps. Thickly, Michael was now cursing Paul, and his face had grown so red that Maureen, who had turned swiftly at the sound of the yell, now advanced anxiously to do something about this latest atrocity of Paul's. A hush had fallen over the party, although the music played on unmindful of the surrounding tension, and weaved out a little drama of its own. "You!" Michael was thickly yelling. And suddenly, now at the height of his rage, he wrapped his hand around the brass stem of the floor lamp next to him and began hoisting it with great effort.

"Look out!" cried Leo, jumping back. Michael had lifted the floor lamp now with both hands and was raising it over his head, trailing the light cord. Paul stood indecisively.

Down came the lamp in a slow but vicious arc, and Paul stepped aside just in time, for on the spot where had had been standing, the lamp, lampshade and bulbs and all now smashed jarringly and hissed and sparked on the floor and went out. The room was plunged in the half darkness of the candlelight, and all the girls had momentarily screamed in terror. And the music played on as indomitably as before.

There was a frantic scuffling as Michael reached out for Paul, who had begun to hurry towards the window of the other room. Michael tripped over the fallen lamp and fell with a crash, precipitating a vase to the floor with him. Paul, now at the window, was raising the sash and letting himself out on the fire escape. Michael was back on his feet—but hands had reached out to restrain him. Shaking them off violently, Michael broke loose and lunged to the window. But Paul had disappeared, and Michael, panting with emotional exhaustion, now fell to his knees and leaned his elbows wearily on the windowsill.

"What? What? What?" Barbara kept sobbing, while Leo and Arthur and Hubert were anxiously hovering behind Michael, who was staring down from his station at the windowsill, at the next landing of the fire escape.

"Good Lord!" Leo was panting, "what's all this damned business!? Stop it, will you, the both of you? You're crazy, the both of you!"

"My lamp!" Maureen suddenly cried from the other room, and Toni was forced to giggle.

"But Paul's not gone," Arthur now said wondrously, for he had leaned over Michael's head and was looking down. "He's on the flight of the fire escape below."

Paul was sitting on the landing below, looking up calmly at Michael, who, kneeling at the window, was looking down with equal calm.

Michael motioned his hand at Paul and said, gently, almost sorrowfully, "Go away."

Paul was silent. Then he stood up and grasped the handrail. Across the apartment building court, some windows were opening, and people were looking up and down the darkness trying to fathom the mystery of the noise.

"You feel like sending everybody home, don't you?" Paul said, still looking up calmly at the fellow who had just tried to brain him. "But you don't know how. Love or hate, you're a failure."

"Go away," Michael repeated, as gently and sorrowfully as before.

Arthur was so amazed at all this, he wouldn't budge from the window as Leo tugged at his sleeve so that he too could witness the strange scene. Julius had gone to the other window and was opening it.

Paul began to descend the fire escape. Then, pausing once again, he looked up at Michael through the framework of the bars. "The moon," he pronounced, pointing up at the sky. "Why don't you fly to it?"

Michael didn't answer, and Paul descended the remaining flight and was soon dissolved into the darkness of the alley below.

Michael then got up and walked across the two rooms under the scrutiny of all the eyes. He went into his room and closed the door quietly. There was a hush—followed by many mumbles of excitement and curiosity, and finally, the murmur of departure. The party was quietly breaking up and everybody was going elsewhere.

Maureen put on her coat and went out with the others. She confessed that she was afraid of Michael—at least, for this night—and that she wouldn't sleep there at all costs; and Barbara extended her an invitation to stay at her place for the night. So that Michael was left alone in the apartment that night, with the broken lamp left as it lay—and with whatever thoughts he had.

WHEN MAUREEN RETURNED to her apartment the following day, she found a note from Michael stating that he would be gone for awhile, perhaps a week or so, on a trip south. He had packed a small bag.

Michael had the habit of going off on short trips, especially when he began to feel the pressure of his own nervous tension, so that Maureen was not too alarmed at his absence. He always came back.

Paul, too, had disappeared from the campus scene. Leo was of the opinion that he, for all that had happened, was probably gone for good. No one as yet understood the full significance of the violent scene at the party, with its touching and gentle denouement, so that the absence of both "participants" tended to reduce interest in the mysterious affair to a minimum.

A third absence was noted around the general campus neighborhood, that of both Anthony and Marie. Arthur, who had grown accustomed to plenty of excitement, now felt suddenly becalmed; and though he was immersed in his studies of that week, he waited with some impatience for the return of Michael, or even of Paul or Anthony, for life was certainly not the same without these tempestuous beings.

And so one day, Paul returned—exactly a week after Spring Day eve—and it was Leo who found him sitting on a bench in the park. It was a rather gloomy, gray-skied, ominous day full of the smell of rain and thawing spring muds.

"Where have you been, Paul?" cried Leo happily, looking anxiously into his friend's face. "I thought you were gone for good."

"I knew you would think that," Paul answered, smiling and blushing. "Well, how are you, Leo?"

"All right. Where did you go?"

"Just out of the city for a while."

"To do what?" Leo persisted.

"Come on," Paul ignored his questioning. "Let's go straightaway to Michael's. I was going there myself, but now that you're here, we'll go together . . ."

Leo glanced sharply at the other.

"Do you think Michael will want to see you?" he asked, remembering all too clearly the incident of the floor lamp.

"Certainly. He'll have forgotten about everything. Don't you even know Michael at all?"

They walked up X Street. "Michael's been gone all this time, too," Leo told Paul. "They say he took a trip south. And where did you go? . . . what did you do?"

"Well, if you insist on knowing . . . I just went on a little excursion through the country. That's all."

They were going up the stairs at Michael's apartment when they met Maureen coming down with a shopping bag under her arm. She seemed to be in a hurry. "Well," was the first thing she said. "Michael's going to be glad to see you!" She paused and glanced at Paul's clothes. "You might as well give it up anyway. Michael's not back from his trip yet. Why do you insist on bothering him?"

"It's none of your business," said Paul evenly. Maureen shrugged her shoulders and went down the stairs; they heard the hall door alarm as she went out. Paul continued on up the stairway and walked carelessly into Maureen's apartment; he went to the front room and flung himself on the couch. "Where are you, Leo?" he called.

Leo walked into the apartment indecisively. "What are we going to do here?" he asked. "I don't think Maureen will like it!" He stood over the couch and looked down at Paul.

"You noticed the door wasn't locked, didn't you?" Paul said to him. "It's fairly an invitation, my friend. But I had a purpose in wanting to come up here . . . What was it? Oh, yes! Poetry."

"What?"

Paul went into Michael's bedroom and began going through the workdesk drawer. "Ah," he said, holding up several sheets of paper. "At last. This has been my first opportunity to take these."

Leo, with his head in the doorway—a picture of reluctant eagerness—asked, "What are they?"

"They're Michael's writings, some of them, at least."

Paul stuffed the papers in his pockets and started to walk out of the apartment. "Come on," he beckoned to Leo. "Let's go out now."

"What's Michael going to say about your walking into

his bedroom and stealing his writings? He'll be so mad all over again, only worse!"

Paul was laughing.

"Are you going to keep them?" Leo inquired.

"If I like them."

They were down on the street again. Paul, who had stopped, was looking up at the dark cloudy sky and sniffing the air. "What a terrible day," he shuddered. "And yet there's energy in the air. It may be a day of power."

They walked on up X Street. "Well," Leo concluded. "That was a neat bit of lifting. Now what are you going to do with his poetry?"

"Read it." Paul was already reading a page as he walked.

"Is that all you did," Leo asked, smiling at Paul, "on your excursion, sleep on the grass and eat fruit for breakfast? Hey?"

"That's enough, isn't it?" Paul said. "It was beautiful, you know. Will you look at this," he added, waving a paper at Leo. "Listen. I'll read you a line or two here: 'Symbols pristine and splendorous I need, for my journey down this corridor: here, now, too late to rejoin the others, and accident need not apologize.' Foo! As though accident apologized for anything! What utter rot he writes!"

"What is he talking about?" Leo asked, leaning over to look at the paper. "Symbols, corridors . . ."

ORPHEUS EMERGED

"And here's some more," Paul went on, ignoring Leo's question. " 'I am high—I reprise my sympathy for the masses.' More nonsense—he won't call a spade a spade, the masses indeed! He means his family, of course. That's the rotten part about all this business, this poetry. Oh! And look here: 'On the other side of this corridor, across these obstructions inviting insanity, I see new emotions and a new humanity: a cultural emotional, ultimacies, new man, shadows of this grotesque deformity: Beauty is tyrant, passion overrules; this instinct is mute, this vision Eternal.' You see, don't you, Leo, that when he cannot express what he means, he says 'this instinct is mute' and such trash. Ultimacies . . . Now as to that, I don't know. Cultural emotionals . . . Yes. Hmm. I only criticize what I understand, of course. Those points there, they may be of course way beyond my learning. Michael is a very learned fellow . . ."

Leo began to laugh and had to stop short in the midst of their walking. "Really, Paul, you make me laugh. First you call Michael a dunce and a fool, and the next moment you dub him as 'very learned.' He's neither, you know. You should learn to control your excesses—"

"Yes? Well, then, if that's so, what does this mean: 'Mind the basis of Eternity.' Now what on earth is that if it isn't profound and learned? Mark you, Leo, I only criticize those parts of the work that I understand. But there are places where Michael is far beyond me . . ."

Leo was still laughing.

" 'Mind the basis of Eternity,' " repeated Paul almost angrily. "Explain that if you will, Professor!"

"It wouldn't be difficult," gasped Leo faintly, "if I had knowledge of his special vocabulary, or even if I read the whole poem. You can be so charmingly naïve—really, it's amazing to watch."

Paul was thumbing through some other pages . . . now, he cried out exultantly, "And this! This I expected to find, by all means! Listen: 'One October feeling is worth ten archetypal tragedies that occur beneath the tender blue char of morning skies: and one melancholy frowse of harvest stack, now, beyond measure surpasses this news of human travail.' Don't you see, in order to speak with God—as he puts it—he's trying to dehumanize himself. Claims here October moves him more than news of human tragedy."

"That's interesting."

"And now, to cap all the nonsense, is this despairing cry!" Paul went on excitedly. "'*Quelqu'un a derange ma noirceur*! This I scream to a deaf and dumb cosmos.' That's nice, isn't it Leo, but yet so typical of the stupid poet. 'Someone has disturbed my darkness,' he cries in French. Why on earth in French? His darkness indeed! That's why he will sleep at all times of the day and night, and dream. What was that I heard a few weeks ago in class? Someone was talking about it . . . the death-instinct, the death-instinct of Freud . . .”

“Perhaps.”

“And he adds here, rather sulkily, 'better to live in hell than to die in heaven.' Does he claim it was heaven before? . . . ha ha! Then he admits it . . .”

“What on earth are you talking about?” Leo now inquired impatiently.

“All esoteric matters,” Paul said. “And look at this!”—he had found more lines to read—“ ‘Alone with no one to love, is hell alive: can I not wait for bunglers and stumblers that straggle out to me? Here, as at the end of a telescope, a crater of the moon. I wait for one of my kind with whom to wallow in my kindness.' Now that,” Paul scoffed, “is sheer nonsense. He's trying to work up the reader's pity, or God's. And he adds: ‘Aesthetic hell, I'm home.' Ho ho! That's good . . . he knows more about himself than he cares to admit. Calls it a ‘sordid denouement.' But here, his hope is regained; he says, ‘Tell me—for my emotions have always been, since then, but shifting sand—tell me that this is Eternity, the Sphinx and not the sand.' What does he think he's found? Is he panting after the new vision too, like all the others? Ha ha ha.”

"I swear," Leo said, "I've never heard anything like your criticism. Why don't you do it objectively? It's terrible to walk with you and hear you defame the work of a man which you've just stolen."

"I'll go one better," Paul laughed, leering at Leo. "I'll burn the whole works—what would you think of that?"

"What? You mean, what would he think of that! You're being very stupid, by the way; I don't think you understand what he's saying . . ."

"Oh, yes!" cried Paul. "I understand better than he does. Look! He bases the whole long poem on a line from one of his dreams. Here, on the first page, it says 'from a dream—' and the quotation, taken, you see, from a dream he had, reads like this: 'Is this the way I'm supposed to feel?' Don't you see, Leo, he's searching for a new emotion, since he has rejected the one he had before. So first he disclaims the old emotion by saying, am I supposed to feel it anyway? Then . . . at the end of the poem, after a thorough exploration of his so-called new emotion and new vision, which is some sort of mystical solipsism undergone in a 'dark corridor'—perhaps a symbolism from a dream—he finds that his journey into these regions, across this corridor, has been a failure. It reads: 'This corridor alone remains—this corridorial loneliness.' Now, I admit that all this is lovely and appealing to the eye, to some extent, but it's failure altogether."

"You may be right," Leo put in, "but still it's no reason for you to burn it. And I want to read these some time."

"Failure altogether," Paul continued, ignoring Leo's remarks. "He finds that there is no new emotion, or if there is, that it's denied to him at least. Like that fellow Rimbaud that Arthur is always talking about. I was thinking about this Rimbaud all the past week."

"Paul," said Leo warmly, "you're the most unusual fellow! Is that what you were thinking about on your bed of grass as you munched your fruit?"

"Perhaps," Paul laughed. "That and many other things, I admit. Now, let's look at a few more of these things. This one is called 'Song of My Modern Sorrow.' A likely title! He has a flair for attracting the eye! Look, that first line explains his whole failure—let's sit down here and I'll read you this . . . "

They were now in the middle of the campus green, and sat on a bench. Immediately, a flurry of pigeons swarmed around them.

" 'Happiness is dead!' he cries straight off. There is the root of his failure—I'll explain. He goes on—'Imponderable sorrow now rules, now stretches its moody nether-glow across my life, my city, and my soul. In the cities, silence mutters smokily. This is the Black Age.' Ho-ho! Now he really is down in the dumps, the Black Age he calls it. First having failed to find a new emotion, the foolish artist turns on his age and attacks it indiscriminately. And listen to this: 'Beauty, now dead, we have enshrined on public squares; and twice daily, queues of dark-shawled women come to weep at the tombstone of joy.' My, my, such sadness! 'There is a child I hear weeping in the steel tunnel beneath the street; and on the street above, a crowd is congregated beholding mutilation, as it rains.' That is rather strange, isn't it, Leo? —I like it, but as they say, I can see all this a little too crystal clear. For instance, this: 'Life is an unpleasant sensation—' like a toothache, ha ha!" Paul inserted wildly. "And then it says, 'knowledge is the enchantress of sorrow, and the mood of death.' That's rather nice. 'For the sun has gone out,' he goes on to say, 'and small fires rage on rooftops: and in the north, sieged cities leave their dead on the frozen boulevards. Gardens are brown and bare, and birds are gone forever south: the wounded sparrow peers out of ferret eyes from his nest of corpse hairs in the eave of the Public Library.' "

Paul lowered the sheets. "Oh, what terrible stuff!" he cried. "But as I say, I understand it all too well. And maybe, maybe it moves me."

"I've seen other things that Michael has written," Leo put in at this point, "which are perhaps better than this. Didn't you read his poem on the impulse of God?"

"I may have it here, but I'll have to read it before I listen to anyone praise it. Michael is a failure, I tell you!"

"Why do you keep insisting that?" Leo demanded.

Paul didn't answer. Now he was holding up another sheet and reading it. "Here it is," he said, "I think this one here is the poem that you were just talking about. Hmm, let's see . . . he entitles it, 'Notes Gleaned From a Voyage to Morphina' . . . Morphina, Morphina? Where's that?"

"Well," Leo said, "it should be clear to you. It's a mythical land, the land you go to when you take morphine. De Quincey and his opium, he went there, and all the others like him. It's the *paradis artificial* of Baudelaire . . ."

"And so Michael has been taking to drugs?" Paul asked innocently.

"He's not an addict," Leo assured him. "Under the influence, you see, of drugs, he's managed to discover a new poetic idea—if such one can call it. Here, let me have that paper . . . I'll read you the poem. I've read it before."

Leo took the paper from Paul's hand. Paul reached into his pocket and pulled out a handful of peanuts, which he threw at the pigeons surrounding their bench.

"Here's the way it goes," Leo said, beginning to read.

" 'Contemplate the universe—close your eyes—and, like God, begin to sense, without words or image, sound or shape, the impulse of all creation. This is the pure moment of God's imagination before the epileptic fit of fault and history begins.' "

"That," interrupted Paul, "that is rather strange, and I don't understand it."

"Wait. Now . . . 'A white rhythm underlines the impulse that is soon to issue Logos—The impulse of creation is the key to the sign of the Macrocosm: it is the silence of the Golden Age, the stasis of the soul in repose. I am about to go up in a consuming flame—I am an old saint—and soon I will disappear!' "

"What?" cried Paul incredulously. "Does he say that in all seriousness? Oh, the folly of all this . . ."

"Never mind," Leo warned him, and continued to read. " 'I feel everything, I sense God, and I exist with Eternity. I have lost my human self: I am one with Paramatma! Listen!—silence rings its immortal chord . . .' "

But Paul had jumped up on his feet and was pacing nervously back and forth in front of the bench.

" 'In the middle of creation, in an attitude of silence and cunning, with my hands over my eyes and ears, I think, I feel, I pray to the mute darkness of my soul, I wait, I hold my breath, and now, slowly, softly, all meaning marches to me, and God is on the threshold of my being, and is soon to enter me, and become One with me! Then! . . . I open my eyes, uncover my ears, and breathe, and there is the sky on the pool atremble, here is the birdsong and the murmur, the morning-moist grass—clean as the rain on dark tree-trunks—and an odor from the meadow beyond where the cows stand mute, and a crow caws and the forest roof reverberates. I know what the flower is, just after the break of sun! I know with God! . . .' "

Paul came back and sat down on the bench beside Leo.

"He can't!" he was mumbling. "He should realize that—"

"Look!" cried Leo, who had been reading another part of the sheet. "This is strange! Can it be? . . . look what he wrote here. 'This is an age that has created sick men like me—' "

"The age again!" Paul scoffed impatiently. "Age! Age! Completely absolved of all responsibility to himself, isn't he! . . ."

" 'What we need is a journey to new lands. I shall embark soon on one of these. I shall sleep on the grass and eat fruit for breakfast.' Now, isn't that what you just told me a while ago, isn't that what you did? How can he have— But I know, when you knew each other in the past, it was a stock phrase between the two of you, isn't that it?"

"Nothing of the sort!" cried Paul, almost angrily.

"But of course! Unless it's a famous line from some other poet. No? How can it be? You said that very same thing just a few minutes ago, you told me you had slept on the grass and eaten fruit for breakfast, don't you remember? Maybe it's that . . . yes, you've obviously read this poem before, and you were quoting his lines . . ."

"No," said Paul gravely, "no, not at all."

"But that's impossible!" Leo cried.

"Oh, is it?" Paul replied, again getting up nervously from the bench. "No, Leo, I assure you: The same phrase happened to enter his mind."

"Nonsense."

"And why shouldn't it be possible? Who are you to deny it! It's very simple . . ."

"It's not so simple," Leo answered firmly.

"It is!" Paul fairly screamed. "You don't know the facts . . . Oh shut up!" And with this, Paul had started to walk away; then he came back and wrenched the papers from Leo, who was grinning at the angry Paul. At this point Arthur hove into sight around the walk.

"Well, Paul," he greeted. "You're back . . ."

"Where are you going?" Leo inquired of Arthur.

"I'm on my way to Michael's. I just saw Julius, and he told me that Michael was back from his trip."

"He's not home. We just went there."

"He's home now. Here comes Julius now, he'll tell you." And with this, Arthur hurried on to Michael's house. Julius was coming up the walk in his slow, leisurely gait.

"Hello, Paul!" he called. Paul, with the papers in his pockets, was walking away from Leo. "Wait a minute!" called Julius, hurrying his pace.

"Well?" said Paul defiantly. "What do you want, Julius?"

Julius stopped and began smiling at Paul. "I have a little news for you," he said. "About Michael's so-called trip . . ."

"What of it?"

"Yes," pressed Leo, "tell us."

"You might as well know," Julius began, "since it's all beginning to come out. This past week, Michael, on his so-called trip, has really been living in the Bohemian Quarter with Anthony's wife, Marie . . ."

"What?" Paul gasped.

"Yes. And they say that Anthony is all out of sorts, because Marie had just left him a note, and didn't explain where she was going or why. The truth was, she went on a little holiday with our Michael, they've been having an affair down in the Quarter . . ."

"And you say that Anthony is . . .?" Paul stammered. "He's ill, I heard. From the shock, they say; but I happen to know that it's mostly from drink. With Marie gone, he just let himself go and drank and drank, and the reason why no one's seen him all this past week is because he's been stay-ing in his room drinking and starving himself. Both Michael and Marie just came back a half an hour ago. I just saw Michael on X Street, and he told me that Marie had gone to her place to tend to the derelict husband . . ."

"You seem to be happy about it all!" Paul accused, for Julius was saying all this in a tone of great relish.

Julius held up his hands, as though to say, 'What do I care? These are the tribulations of others—and they amuse me.'

"Well!" Leo said at length, and fell into a daze of reflec-tion.

"I was the first to know all about this affair," Julius went on, with a faint smile on his face. "You see, I was down in the Quarter about five days ago, and I saw Michael and Marie walking across the Quarter Park. I kept everything to myself, of course, but I knew, after I'd seen them down there, what was going on. Michael had stopped to talk to some little children who were playing in the park, and I managed to duck into a doorway and watch to see where they were going. They went into a small apartment house."

"All right, all right!" cried Paul impatiently.

"You seem to resent this news!" Julius said, surprised.

"It's only your attitude," Paul muttered, "although I can

understand that, too." And with this, Paul walked away without any further say.

"Where are you going?" Leo called. "To Anthony's," Paul flung back, and he hurried on. Leo nodded briefly to Julius and started out after Paul.

"Paul," he cried, "I have to go to my class this afternoon. I wish I could go with you!" Paul was in too much of a hurry to answer, so that Leo stopped, gazed rather ruefully after the other, and then turned dutifully around and went to his class.

Paul had reached Marie's apartment house and was climbing the steps when he met her coming down. "Marie!" he said. "I've just heard . . ."

"Yes, yes," she muttered impatiently, pushing him out of the way to pass. Paul persisted and followed her down to the landing.

"But Marie, what's it all about? How's Anthony?"

Marie stopped and glared at Paul. "Will you shut up? It's none of your business. If you insist on being little Jesus Christ, go on up and watch Anthony while I'm out."

"Well, where are you going now?"

"I'm going to see Maureen and I'm going to get some medicine. Is that all you want to know?"

"But this is all so crazy!" Paul cried, holding out his

hands. "I don't understand what you've done . . . and Michael. I mean, why?"

"And you're the craziest of the lot," Marie told him. "Shut up and play your part." And with this, Marie walked out on the street.

Paul stood for at least a whole minute, after that, staring after the vanished Marie. Then he shrugged his shoulders and went upstairs to Marie's apartment.

There, in the bedroom, he found poor Anthony asleep; Marie had obviously put him to bed. The room smelled terribly of liquor and of fever. There were at least five quart bottles of whiskey, all of them empty, strewn around the floor; and dirty clothes abounded on all the chairs. Anthony had obviously been living in this room ever since Marie's departure—in the room, significantly enough, where they slept together as man and wife—and it was evident from the general wreckage around that at first he had flown into a destructive rage and broken furniture and flower pots; and later, when that had died down, he had bought a week's store of liquor and proceeded to annihilate his misery. Paul knew, as he stood there looking down at Anthony, that the wretch had planned his game well; that he knew, when Marie returned, that she would find him there in their marital chamber, a complete wreck. And this, it must be remarked, was Anthony's revenge on

Marie: she would find him in this state, and thus feel guilty about her escapade. It was a perfect martyr-technique.

Paul went back into the front room and sat down by the window. It was growing darker outside with the thickening clouds, and there was the smell of rain in the air.

Marie finally came back, with packages under her arm. Without saying a word to Paul, who, for his part, was also silent, she went to work on her husband. Ice bags, pills, hot soup—everything was marshaled into the devotional labor, and Paul could hear, from his seat in the other room, the cooing sounds of Anthony's revival. "Marie, Marie," he was mumbling. "Why did you do it?"

And Marie only answered, "Shut up!" and marched out of the bedroom with the empty whiskey bottles and threw them in the dumb-waiter.

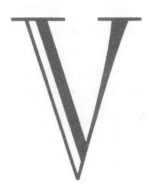

ARTHUR PUSHED OPEN the door of Michael's bedroom and looked in. Michael was sitting in the easy chair by the window, smoking a cigarette and staring gloomily outside at the gray rooftops.

"Michael!" greeted Arthur. "Just got back?"

Michael looked up. "Yes," he said. "How are you, Arthur? Have you seen Maureen?"

Arthur smiled. "Yes, I just saw her down by the markets. She's out shopping, I guess. I don't suppose she knows—"

"Knows what?"

"Well," Arthur began with a half-mocking, half-bashful smile. "I know all about it, I mean your affair with Marie in the Quarter . . ."

Michael seemed startled.

"Our friend Julius happened to see you there a few days ago, well . . . and he told me about it."

Smiling nervously, Michael motioned Arthur to sit on the bed; then he shrugged his shoulders wearily. "I suppose everyone will know in time."

"And moreover," Arthur went on, "Paul is back. He's been away for a spell himself. I saw him just now with Leo in the campus park."

Michael didn't say anything. Quite irrelevantly, he raised his eyebrows and said, "I don't care who finds out about Marie and me. I don't care at all what happens. What have you been doing, Arthur?" Michael extinguished his cigarette in the ashtray on the arm of the chair. He looked very gloomy.

"I've been thinking something out," Arthur said, making himself comfortable on the bed, propping a pillow under his arm and leaning on his elbow. "I want your opinion on these matters. I've prepared a sort of manifesto, let's say, or an essay of a sort. It's on the subject of the artist . . ."

"That's a nonsensical pursuit," smiled Michael.

"Not theoretically. You must admit that much of modern thought is centered around the problem of the artist and society, of the artist and himself—as in Rimbaud, for instance, in his case . . ."

"Yes, I know," admitted Michael disconsolately, "but so many artists are preoccupied with the question, they can't find time to create."

"One sometimes has to clear the decks. Wagner spent years arranging his intellectual system before he could compose. Clearly, also, it is one of the central absorptions of Thomas Mann."

"I admit that."

"Look, Michael . . ." and Arthur extracted a sheet of paper from his pocket. "Here I've worked out a symbolism, a modern one that is . . . ah, applicable to my system. It's Prometheus! The artist, Prometheus, steals fire from the gods—the fire, the secret, of creation—and brings it down to earth. I admit of course that none of this is original. Rimbaud secured an idea much like it from Ballanche, and I, of course, from Rimbaud. Now you see the system implies much that is Cabalistic, in a sense: you know, to stand on the threshold of vegetable life facing God and sharing his secrets, as in Blake also. You! You, for instance, fit into the symbolism—as Prometheus, the thief of divine fire. I've read your poetry. In it, I find that you are attempting to speak with the impulse of God . . . in that poem, 'Morphina' for instance. I'm beginning to see what you're after, but I have here something further for you . . ."

"I, Prometheus?" asked Michael almost angrily.

"As a symbol—"

"I know. But when I could be *Orpheus!* Have you ever looked into that? There's a symbol for you!"

"What do you mean?"

"Orpheus! Orpheus!" shouted Michael. Then he relapsed once more to his shy smile. "Oh this is all nonsense."

"Tell me."

"Well, you say that the artist—in this case, myself—you say that I am a plausible symbol of Prometheus. Prometheus the artist, when I could be Orpheus, the *artist-man!* Do you understand what I'm trying to say? When I could be the whole artist *and* man. Unchained! you see—for Prometheus is chained to a rock, God knows—unwounded, unlike Cocteau's poet, or Henry James' artist; unsevered, Arthur, unsevered!"

"You'll have to explain."

"I fear that it will all be clear to you anyway before long. A chain of events and not my words will illumine the meaning. Ah, but I'm tired . . ."

"Never mind that. In those poems that you completed I found—"

"Completed!" interrupted Michael. "But I've never completed anything."

"How could you then account for ever having created anything?"

"I don't know. That's how I feel. The pathways of creation are devious."

"Well," said Arthur, "I still don't follow you. You sound incoherent."

"I mean—Well perhaps I have completed something. There are the parts, and since these parts are in themselves complete, then there must exist somewhere a complete whole."

"Precisely," said Arthur wearily, as though he had wanted to explain this all along, and was impatient to continue with what he was saying. "Now, the artist—"

"The artist! The artist!" Michael was in a savage mood, and he was constantly pressed to smile, in order to undo his antagonism. "All right, go on. But be careful . . ."

"Of what?"

Michael turned his eyes to the rooftops again. "I don't know. I sound like a smug father, to tell you that; and God knows, no one is ever old enough to give advice. Well what I mean is be careful of art, as art: if you take it seriously, ultra-seriously, there is liable to be—"

"The consequences are what I crave," Arthur said subtly.

Michael looked at Arthur in surprise.

"We're dissimilar," he concluded, after watching Arthur for several moments. "Perhaps, at least . . .What I mean— and I often wonder if I ever say anything that is anywhere near the point—is that the consequences of espousing art like a *priest*, say, are often—harmful—to the whole man."

"In art I intend to find wholeness," Arthur put in.

"In art," Michael said, "I found halfness."

They were silent, staring at each other. The door suddenly opened and Maureen walked in. Her jaw was trembling, she was pale, and glaring at Michael. There was a shocked silence.

"Get out," she said.

"Well?" Michael began.

"Get out. I just saw that witch Marie down at the markets—and she told me everything."

After a pause, Michael shrugged. "I don't care," he said wearily.

"Get out," repeated Maureen. "I want you to get out." She was holding a bag of provisions under her arm that she'd just been buying before Marie approached her.

"And why?"

"I'll kill you if you don't get out. And you too, young man. Get out with him. All of you are children, and all of your are fools."

Michael laughed.

"Laugh," said Maureen. "Laugh because you're ignorant. Get out. Don't ever come back, it might be dangerous."

"Nay, fatal," Michael mocked.

"Get out," she repeated again quietly. Michael sighed and rose from the chair. "My clothes—"

"I'll pack them and give them to you tomorrow. Get out right away."

Michael and Arthur walked out of the apartment.

"Well," said Arthur as they walked down the stairs and out onto X Street, "does that mean the end of your affair with Maureen? I guess it does," he concluded himself.

"Yes," sighed Michael. He seemed a little weary; even the menacing scene with Maureen had not succeeded in bringing him out of his indolent ennui. "It was convenient while it lasted."

Arthur gave Michael a slanting glance. "Is that all you can say?"

Michael sighed again and didn't answer. They walked along across the campus. Presently, he said, "That's all the situation warrants."

Arthur, a trifle embarrassed, repressed an impulse to express his feelings for Maureen and for her position in the matter. It had been fairly evident to him, that to Maureen, the affair had held more meaning than could be encompassed in Michael's bland use of the word "convenient."

"Now—" Michael said, falling deeper and deeper into his gloominess, "Now, I suppose it's time to go to Marie's."

"Why?"

"She *is* a witch, that Marie," Michael reflected tiredly. "There was no need to tell Maureen everything. What can hurt a woman like Maureen more than to tell her to her face that her lover has been made the victim of a conquest—"

"Well, hardly."

"I suppose," Michael droned on, "that Marie is the type who does a good job, a thorough job, of things when she transgresses . . ."

Arthur almost laughed. "Strange talk! Transgression! Now you're no longer the artist beyond good and evil, but a sinner in arms . . ."

"You must admit it's hard to purge your system of the notion," Michael mumbled. "I knew a man once who had himself psychoanalyzed in order to get rid of the notion, and to be happy: good and evil, he didn't care one way or the other. Good and evil blur your vision—God doesn't make the distinction, you know. You can't rid yourself of it . . . especially when you're a human being. Biologically speaking, I'm afraid all poetic vision is rot."

"Now, now," Arthur leered, "don't let little things let you down."

Arthur laughed to conceal his confusion on the matter. They had crossed the campus, and now they were walking down the boulevard in the direction of Marie's house.

"It's going to rain soon," Michael observed. "It's the end . . ."

Paul was sitting in Marie's front room when they arrived there, with his head leaning on his hand, and staring fixedly into space. When he saw Michael and Arthur, he looked up and smiled, but said nothing.

Marie came out of the bedroom carrying a towel and stopped short on seeing Michael.

"Well?"

"Nothing," mumbled Michael. "I only came to see you about your telling Maureen. It wasn't necessary, you know."

"It wasn't necessary!" mimicked Marie savagely. "Shut up, won't you, and go home." She brushed past Michael and Arthur and went into the kitchen.

"Well? Was it?" cried Michael, following her. Marie did not answer. Michael came back and dropped himself wearily on the couch. He stared dully at Paul across the room.

"And where have *you* been?" he demanded sullenly.

"I heard that while you were in the Bohemian Quarter—that is, when Julius saw you," Paul rushed on to say, heedless of the question, "and according to his version, of course, that you stopped to talk to some children in the park—that was the way he put it—"

"Well, what of that?"

"I'm only referring to the incident he described where you stopped to talk to some children . . ."

"All right, all right!" cried Michael impatiently. "What are you saying?"

"Just—thank you."

There was a silence, during which Arthur seemed bewildered at all this. Michael only tilted his head to one side and gave Paul a grave and scornful glance.

Marie was back, crossing the room. "I'll have no loud talking and yelling. All of you had best go home, anyway. You're of no use here."

Michael followed her into the bedroom. Anthony was peacefully asleep, with just the hint of a smile on his lips.

"What a big baby!" Michael exclaimed softly. Marie turned to him and almost smiled. But solemnly she said, "And what do you think you are?"

"I'm not a baby."

"Hmm?"

Marie lowered the windowpane, arranged Anthony's blankets, motioned Michael out of the room, and quietly closed the door. She went over to a desk drawer and took out a cigarette and lit it.

Arthur, of course, was very embarrassed and uncomfortable; particularly now since Michael and Marie had ceased to harangue with one another: the situation warranted some haranguing, else how account, in moral terms, for the derelict in the next room. But Marie seemed quite calm with her cigarette, and Michael seemed to have forgotten his anger over the Maureen matter. Paul, for his part, though betraying no signs of discomfort, had lapsed again into a preoccupied contemplation of space. The first raindrop spat against the windowpane. Marie went to the lamp and turned it on. The evening had come on within the space of a raindrop and the click of a lamp.

"Well?" Marie said, for none of the three youths had spoken. Arthur looked with some desperation towards Michael, then to Paul.

Michael got up from the couch. "I guess I'll go home," he said. Paul made no move to rise from his chair.

"Do you still want to know why I told Maureen?" Marie asked.

Michael shrugged. "I guess I know. Yes, I do know. But I think it was stupid on your part—you want to flagellate yourself, complete the picture; but Maureen, well, what about her?"

Marie was laughing. "Discounting what you just said about flagellation, what are you supposed to care about people's feelings, according to what you told me in the Quarter?"

Marie was watching Michael intently. Paul, too, was now watching.

"Suppose," Michael said wearily, "suppose I wanted the freedom to care when I wanted to, and not to care when I didn't?"

"*That's* complicated!" Marie mocked, blowing smoke towards Michael.

"Oh, is it?" sneered Michael, and turned away.

"You're a fool," Marie added slowly.

"You're frank at least," he answered. "I don't mind your being frank. But you don't belong to this world: if you allege yourself tied to it, why don't you act accordingly?"

"Does that confuse you?"

"Yes, yes!" yelled Michael suddenly. "Oh, why don't you leave me alone!"

"Ha ha ha!" shouted Paul from his chair in the corner.

"And you!" Michael cried, turning to Paul. "Why don't

you go back to your wet grass and your fruits!"

"Oh, you know about that?" Paul inquired archly.

Michael threw up his hands. "It's the way you all think you understand my every next move. It's completely disgusting. Don't you know what a spectacle you all make of yourselves? You and that Julius . . ."

"What on earth are you talking about?" Marie inquired.

"You know damned well what I'm talking about, but that's beside the point, I suppose, in that damned pattern of yours!"

"Pattern?"

"Ha ha ha!" shouted Paul again from his chair.

Michael gave him a seething look. Paul put in quickly, "I know what you're thinking! Traitor! Traitor! Oh, what a joke that one is! By the way, did you know that I stole your poetry today?"

Michael didn't seem to have heard, or if he had, he didn't seem to care.

Paul took out some papers and waved them at Michael. "Shall I read you some excerpts, hey?"

"To hell with all of you!" Michael said grimly. "I'm wasting my time here." And suddenly he had hurried to the door, and they heard it open and slam hard.

"Don't get lost in your corridor!" Paul yelled after him, jumping up from his chair and going to the door. A moment later he was back, and sat down in his chair and started to laugh.

Marie walked towards him and stopped to look down at him.

"You can be very mean," she said. "Do you know that?"

"I'm talented," Paul said.

"Hmm."

Arthur was standing indecisively. It had begun to rain steadily outside, and the window drummed and rattled in the wind.

"It seems superfluous to have to be mean to a person who doesn't know how to be happy," Marie went on.

Paul looked up at her, surprised. "You think that of Michael, that he can't be happy?"

"He doesn't know how. We were miserable in the Quarter."

"And as for myself? Do I know how to be happy?"

"Yes."

"It's interesting that you should know that," Paul said quickly.

"Just why?"

"That is the main point about Michael," Paul rushed on. "He himself thinks otherwise, I mean as to the point: he's always preoccupied with his so-called amorality, and just because of that simple fact, he's *not* amoral—but he doesn't know that, does he? No, the point about Michael is rather that he doesn't know how to be happy."

"Well," Arthur ventured, as he moved towards the door. "I think I'll be going now, to dinner. Is anyone going to dinner?"

"Not now," Marie said.

"Well, good night," said Arthur, and went out.

"Arthur's a nice fellow," Paul said dreamily, "but he takes Michael much too seriously."

They were silent as the rain and wind beleaguered the windowpane.

"Did you enjoy your escapade?" Paul inquired at length as he lit himself a cigarette.

"Not too much."

"Does Michael's inferiority complex annoy you?"

"It did."

"Would you do it again?"

"Perhaps—but not with him. It was somewhat pleasant, though."

"You're a strange girl, Marie; way beyond my comprehension, too."

Marie laughed scornfully and turned on the radio.

"Good-bye," said Paul, getting up from the chair. "I wish you could meet Helen when she comes here some day. You're the nearest thing to Helen I've seen in my life."

"Is that a compliment?"

"It's by way of being a compliment from both Michael and myself."

"Oh?"

Paul laughed nervously. "I'll bet you're thinking of me as a little fool. Well enough, I don't care: it doesn't bother me. Good-bye, Marie."

Marie nodded and Paul went out.

MICHAEL, ON THE STREET outside of Marie's apartment, huddled up in his coat and turned up the collar to the rain. He started to walk, hardly caring in what directions his footsteps took him. But a vague idea was forming in the back of his mind, and he began to hurry towards the Boulevard Bar.

Three men were coming down the sidewalk in Michael's direction. They wore raincoats and were shouting and singing in a carefree manner. As they approached Michael, they formed a wedge in the center of the sidewalk and were quiet. Michael, intent on his destination, and with his head lowered against the driving rain, walked straight up to them expecting in any event that they would make room for him, since they occupied the entire sidewalk. But they did not separate, and one of them suddenly waved his arms and began yelling, "Out of my way! Out of my way, everybody!" And saying this, he bumped directly into Michael, pushed him aside violently with his elbow, and paused to stare at him questioningly, with a look of stupefaction on his face. The other two men began to laugh. Michael registered only mild astonishment, since he was so preoccupied with his anger against Marie and Paul, and it hardly occurred to him that his person was being insulted—at least, for the moment.

The three men laughed as Michael shuffled on in the rain.

And just as Michael reached the top of the street and was turning into the boulevard, he heard the men shouting, followed by the shattering of glass.

He turned in time to see the three men, laughing uproariously, run away from the street level window of an apartment house that they had just broken with a volley of rocks.

Michael stopped, stunned and frightened. Then he hurried on up the boulevard towards the bar and walked in quickly. It was warm and cheery in the bar, and the place was already filling up despite the dinner hour. Michael sat at a table in the corner, flapped off the rain from his coat collar, and ordered Pernod and water. He looked at his hand and it was trembling violently. When his drinks came, he drank up quickly and began to shiver and tremble all over.

The seaman who had bought Anthony drinks a week ago was standing at the bar talking to two men. He was very drunk again, and occasionally he would totter and almost fall on his back.

"Someday," he was crying thickly—and so loudly that the bartenders were looking at each other with significance—"someday I'm going to walk into a rich man's house, with my dirty boots covered with mud, and with a gun, I'll shoot everything down, the rich man, the paintings on the wall, the expensive vases, the draperies . . . Gentlemen," he went on ponderously, and reeling back against another man who was just then crossing the room, "I shall bring his house down upon his head."

The man into whom the drunken seaman had reeled

now gave a violent push, for he too was drunk, and was annoyed in that someone should reel against him. The seaman went hurtling against the bar, and like a rubber ball, with his crossed eyes gleaming at two divergent points in space, he bounded back into the annoyed drunkard and knocked him to the floor. The drunkard got to his feet immediately and floundered wildly towards the seaman. There was a flurry of waving arms, and suddenly the seaman went down under the impact of an elbow in his face and smashed his head against the brass rail running along the base of the bar. Blood was spewing from the drunkard's nose as he panted, and he now jumped down upon the prostrate seaman and began to pummel his head with his forearms. The two bartenders had by now vaulted over the bar, and in doing so, had overturned a bottle of beer which went crashing to the floor and precipitated a scream from a drunken woman at the corner of the bar.

In a moment, after much violent hauling and pushing, the bartenders had directed the two combatants to the door of the bar and hurled them out into the rain. The patrons of the bar now assembled at the plate glass window, in one excited group, and watched the resumption of the battle outside. There was much shouting, and cries of amazement on the part of the spectators.

"Look at that! Look!"

"He's going to kill him!" a woman cried anxiously, dropping her glass to the floor.

"He's beating his head on the pavement!"

Michael lowered his head and quickly gulped his Pernod. It burned violently in his throat, and he took water. The spectators were still yelling. Michael buried his face in his hands, and suddenly, not to his very great surprise, he had begun to shake violently and even to sob a little. Then he began to feel dizzy and sick; he rose waveringly from the table and rushed to the lavatory. He was there for what seemed an eternity.

When he got back to his table, quiet reigned again in the barroom. They were saying that some policemen had come along and broken up the fight with their billy clubs, and carried the combatants away in their police cars. The spectators were back at their stations along the bar, ordering more drinks. One bartender, with a gleam in his eye as he shook the mixer, was shouting down the bar to the other bartender, "Well! That's it for tonight!"

Michael ordered another Pernod and water and drank it as soon as it came. Now he no longer felt like weeping; he felt only bitterness, and there was a fuzz before his eyes. His hands were still trembling and little drops of sweat were running down into his collar.

After drinking down the third Pernod, Leo was suddenly standing beside his table, carrying a load of books and looking contented.

"Michael!" he greeted. "It's good to see you again!" He sat down and placed his books on the table. "I'm going to drink a glass of beer."

"How are you?" Michael inquired gloomily.

"Fine. But you don't look so well. You're pale, and there's sweat all over your face. Did you know that Paul was back also? I thought you were all gone for good; I was getting lonesome."

Michael smiled wanly.

"I heard a man was just killed," Leo went on, beckoning to the waiter.

"What?"

"Weren't you around ten minutes ago? You missed it. Two men were fighting in here and then out on the sidewalk, and some policemen came along to break it up, and killed one of the men with their billy clubs."

"Are you sure?"

"That's what they're all saying. I saw them carry the dead man into the police car as I came down the boulevard. Tell me, where's Paul?"

Michael was running his hand over his face in great agitation. Looking up quickly, he asked, "Paul?"

"Yes, where is he?"

"I don't know, I don't know."

Leo smiled reassuringly. "You're in a nervous mood, I see. Is it because of the repercussions of the Marie affair?"

"How did you find out? And I don't care, anyway."

"They're saying that Maureen has cast you out, and that Anthony almost died of grief and neglect and alcohol, and all kinds of things."

"Well, what of it?"

"And," Leo went on garrulously, "you'd better ask Paul for your poetry. I was with him today when he stole it, and he threatened to burn it."

"I don't care," Michael said. "God," he added, "I don't care about anything any more. This is the end. Pah!"

Leo laughed loudly. The waiter set the glass of beer before him and Leo took a quick sip.

"I'm going to end my life soon," Michael added suddenly.

Leo laughed more loudly than before. "Now, now," he mocked indulgently. "None of that, and besides, people never mean it when they come out with it that way! Oh, no—remember Ippolit in Dostoyevsky?"

"Ippolit meant what he said," Michael droned, staring into his empty glass. "It wasn't his fault that the gun didn't go off. That part was the biggest tragedy of the book, not what came later."

Leo laughed again; he was in a happy mood, and the

rain had brightened up his usually dour complexion. "I don't take you seriously, at any rate. There's a lot to live for, and you must know that . . ."

Michael didn't answer. He waved to the waiter and ordered another Pernod. Then he turned to Leo: "And you say that one of the men was killed?"

"Yes."

Michael sighed heavily, shakily. "Look at my hands," he said at length, holding them out for Leo to see. "See them shake violently? I'm on the verge of a nervous breakdown. I think I'm going crazy. I've got to put an end to it."

Leo laughed again and squeezed Michael's arm. "Don't be ridiculous. You dramatize everything. A little misery is good for the poet. You yourself wrote this line, I remember it: 'Pain is the law of the artist's life.' Ha ha! Aren't I right?"

Michael shrugged gloomily.

"Pain is the substance of your life. That's what Goethe said. Remember that. Bear it out with fortitude."

"Fortitude!" sneered Michael. "What a dull word!—I'm sick of hearing it. I don't want to be courageous, my emotions are against it; I want to be happy."

"Well—" began Leo.

"Shut up!" yelled Michael. The bartenders had begun to look over to their table. "Not so much noise," one of them called, waving his finger.

Michael glowered at the tabletop. Another Pernod came and he threw a large bill on the table.

"You'd better not drink much more Pernod," Leo warned. "You'll be very drunk in a matter of minutes."

"Well? That's precisely what I want. I'm going to obliterate myself, like Anthony did, but I'm going to do it first with Pernod, and then—"

Michael left off and drank down a whole glassful of Pernod.

Leo grimaced good-naturedly. Suddenly Michael was sobbing with his face in his hands. "Michael!" cried Leo, with a look of consternation. "Now you've done it! You're so drunk you can't control yourself. I think I'd better take you home!" He put his hand on Michael's shivering shoulder, but the other shook him off petulantly and continued to sob.

"Good Lord!" exclaimed Leo in some embarrassment. He stole a glance down the length of the bar to see if anyone was watching this little scene. "Stop being a baby, will you?" Then he began to laugh nervously. "General *lacrimae rerum* is it? Is that why you're crying, the tears of things? My God, you're making a spectacle of yourself—some people are beginning to watch you. Stop it, Michael . . ."

Michael didn't seem to hear what Leo was saying.

Leo curled his lip a bit scornfully: "You fool," he said.

"Stop being a pampered baby. I've never seen such stickish weakness, such drunkenness. It's not like you at all; when I first knew you—"

"Good Lord!" But Michael went on sobbing, with his face hidden in his trembling hands.

"Everybody's looking at you now," Leo whispered. "Stop it! And do you think they're sympathizing with you? Not on your life!! If you think that, you're certainly a psychotic case—you're just a foolish spectacle, that's about all . . ."

Leo began to be very embarrassed, sitting there with a man who wept into his hands like a woman. He picked up his books tentatively.

"Well," he said, after a pause. "I'm going now. You'd better stop this or they'll throw you out. Come, now, aren't you ever going to stop." Leo rose from his seat. "I'm going now, Michael. Good-bye, Michael."

Michael didn't answer.

Leo hesitated another moment or two and then, bestowing a nervous pat on Michael's quivering shoulder, he walked away somewhat self-consciously. A man was standing near the door as Leo approached it.

He took Leo's arm.

"What's the matter with him over there, that fellow you were sitting with who's crying? Hey? Has someone stolen his lollipop, his itsy-bitsy lollipop? Hey? Is that it . . ."

Leo didn't answer, and, disengaging himself from the man's grip, went out the door.

"That's what it is, isn't it?" the man called after him, and turned back to watch Michael, laughing and shaking his head.

VII

WALKING ALONG THE BOULEVARD, Paul was trying to decide where he should go in order to find Michael. Suddenly, he realized that he must go to his room. Would Michael be there? Most likely. And if not—it was time to go there in any event, and tidy up the room a bit, and perhaps pay another week's rent in advance. Paul still had some of the money that Michael had given him the night of the party; he hadn't spent much during his week in the country. Although Michael had heretofore never visited Paul's room, perhaps he would be there now, tonight. He might also be in some bar getting drunk, a habit of his when things went wrong. Paul decided to go to his room first.

It was raining harder as he turned up M street and strode along beneath the dripping street lamp. Yes— Michael might want to talk to him at last, of that Paul was almost certain. With a mounting feeling of certainty, Paul hurried to his gate and descended the stone steps. Surely enough, the oil lamp was burning in his room, its yellow light fell feebly on the dark puddles outside from underneath the drawn shade.

Paul hastened along the damp hallway and flung open his door.

"Helen!" he cried with joyous wonder.

A tall, dark-haired girl stood in the center of the room. She smiled and held out her hands.

Paul, beside himself with excitement, ran up to Helen and stopped just short of her outstretched hands. He teetered there for a moment, looking incredulously into her face; then, with a sighing smile, he dropped down on his knees and took both of her hands in his and began to kiss them over and over again.

"Get off your knees," Helen cried, blushing. "Don't be a fool."

"Helen darling! Helen darling! I *knew* I had to come here—I *felt* it! When did you arrive?"

"Just a few minutes ago," she replied. "Please get off your knees," and she blushed again charmingly.

Paul rose and led Helen to the couch. Sitting her down slowly, and sitting beside her, he kissed her reverently on the brow, and then buried his face in her hair.

"You've come at last," he whispered. "It's been so long. But I knew you'd come. Oh, God! I'm so happy, so damned happy! Look!" he cried suddenly, jumping up from the couch and pointing to a pile of books on the table. "Guess what? I've been studying and learning all the while, and I've met all sorts of intelligent students, friends of Michael's."

"Have you really been happy?"

"No! No! That, to say that, is to defame this moment. *Now* I'm happy. Oh, Helen," he cried, changing his tone again impulsively, and dropping on the couch beside her. "Now that you've come, now that you've come . . . it will all be over! Say that it will!"

"We'll wait," she said slowly.

"Wait? Wait? For what? . . . For Michael? He never comes here; he hasn't once come to my room. Only once he spoke a friendly word, the night of a party to which I wasn't invited, and he wanted to know if I was going to come anyway. I thought that was the moment then, but nothing happened. And later that night, he gave me money —he still has all that money left he took with him—but he gave it to me scornfully. Helen, it's got to stop; it's got to happen some time!"

"He'll come here tonight," Helen said.

"He may not."

"We'll wait here for him."

"But how can you be sure. Do you feel it, Helen?"

She was silent.

Paul got up and began to stride around the room impatiently. Coming back to Helen, he fell on his knees again and began to kiss her wrists feverishly. "I don't know," he said, looking up at her fearfully, his face distorted in the lamp light. "I don't know, Helen darling . . ."

"Well," Helen assured him, stroking his hair, "I do."

Paul now lapsed into an ecstatic silence. Then he jumped up again and went over to the table. "All these books," he said proudly. Then, taking out a sheaf of papers from his pockets, he threw them on the table. "And these are some of his writings. I think I understand most of them—I criticized them to Leo this afternoon."

"Who's Leo?"

"A very brilliant student we know here at Custos Nostrom University, one of my friends."

"And what have you been doing for a living?" Helen asked. "Give me those papers so I can look at them." Paul brought the papers over. He looked down at his shoes and chuckled. "Well," he said warily, "I started out all right, when I first got here. I had a job running an elevator, up and down, the little children coming home from school at noon, the old ladies with their dogs, the old gentlemen going out for their constitutionals, some of them retired *savants* . . ."

"And?" Helen persisted.

"Well, after a while, I was so busy, I had to quit."

"Busy at what?"

"Well, helping Anthony among other things—he's another wonderful friend of mine, a drunkard but a wonderful soul—and attending classes. Did I tell you? I attended classes like a regular student for awhile, until one day the Professor had to put me out because I got mad over a theory that Arthur was propounding. Arthur is another friend of mine, a bit of a poet."

"Then what did you do for a living, after you quit your job?"

Paul looked at Helen. "As I say—you know, *he* gave me money."

Helen shrugged her shoulders.

"And why not?" Paul wanted to know. "But now!" he

added triumphantly. "Now you're here, and it will be all over at last, won't it?"

"I hope so," Helen whispered. "Come, sit with me some more. Kiss me, you fool—you haven't kissed me on the mouth yet."

Paul ran laughing to Helen and kissed her.

"We'll go back," he whispered savagely, "we'll go back and bask by the river bank, won't we? And you'll prepare lunches . . ."

"Oh," Helen said, laughing, "I hate picnics. You and your picnics!"

"And I've thought of all kinds of wonderful new ideas. Here's what I'd like us to do. We'll spend the whole summer going around in our bare feet, somewhere among the pine trees, not far from the surf. I want to be up in the morning when the first ray of dawn makes the top of the pines crack! And—"

"All right," Helen interrupted happily, "that's enough of your dreaming for now."

"As though these things were impossible!" Paul cried wrathfully. "Who?" he asked. "Who is going to tell me it's impossible! Are you like those other people, like Michael— afraid of being happy?"

"You're talking gibberish," Helen mocked, pulling at Paul's sleeve playfully. "Don't get mad!"

"I *am* mad!" Paul cried. He paced the room. "I want to know where all this meanness of spirit comes from—the world's crazy!" He went over to the table and banged it. Then, changing his attitude again in the flicker of a moment, he came back to Helen and buried his face in her hair. "Do you really think he's coming?"

"I think so, yes."

"You know, he hasn't changed much— he's the same as when he left, only perhaps worse. He's more miserable than ever. He tried to hit me with a floor lamp one night. Helen, this can't go on." They were silent, and they could hear the wind blow outside, and the rain spatter into the street.

"Would you like a sandwich?" Paul asked.

"No, not yet. And your bread is all moldy. Let's lie down and wait."

Helen and Paul embraced each other, with both their heads on the same pillow, and in a few moments, Paul was dozing fitfully. Helen was watching him sadly. After several minutes of droning rain-sounds, Helen heard a step in the hall; there was a knock on the door. Paul jumped up, startled out of a half dream. He went to the door and opened it. Leo was standing in the hall.

"Ah, here you are," Leo said.

Paul said coldly, "Well?"

"I've been looking for you," Leo began uncertainly, in

the face of Paul's morose reception. "I'm on my way to my room to study, and . . .well, I just wanted to tell you that Michael is in the Boulevard Bar, very drunk, and he's weeping and making a complete show of himself . . ."

"Weeping?" Paul cried anxiously. "Why?"

"I don't know," said Leo. "He's just drunk, that's all, and he looks like he's coming down with an illness or some-thing—"

Helen came to the door and looked at Leo. The latter was startled out of his wits, but not quite enough to lose control of the situation.

"Why," he said politely, "how do you do?"

"This is Leo, Helen," Paul said sullenly. "Leo, Helen."

Leo bowed from the waist.

"Good-bye," said Paul, and closed the door in the other's face. "Now," he said, turning to Helen, "what are we going to do? Did you hear what he just said?—Michael's sick, and drunk, and he's crying in the bar. I knew all this busi-ness would break him in time—just today he was cast out of his comfortable little nook with a woman old enough to be his mother."

Helen went over to the table and stood by it reflective-ly. "What were you saying about a woman?" she asked presently.

"He was living with Maureen. Then, when she found

out of another affair, she threw him out . . . And the other girl doesn't want Michael, and he, like a fool, is taking everything seriously. Oh! He has done so many stupid things lately, I'm ashamed of myself!" Paul sat on the couch. Again he asked, "What are we going to do?"

"Do? We'll just wait." Helen sat down beside him.

"I don't see your logic!" Paul cried impatiently.

"There's no logic involved in it," Helen replied calmly. "Let's lie down and wait some more. Get some sleep; you look fearfully worn out."

Paul smiled tenderly. "Oh Helen," he said, "if you only knew how much I love you, if only! All right, I won't be a pest. I'll be quiet, and we'll wait. Everything'll be all right, won't it?"

"Yes, Paul."

Paul stretched out on the couch and placed his head in her bosom. "I'm going to sleep, yes," he told her. "When I wake up, it will be all over, and we'll be together and in love, like before . . . Helen, do you think that Michael's change will affect us? . . . do you think it will be different?"

"Perhaps."

"He wanted to be an artist," Paul said sadly, "and he left. It won't be the same man any more," he added gloomily.

"It might be a better man," Helen said, "if only . . . he will come."

They again fell into a long, peaceful silence. Helen was stroking Paul's hair; her own long dark hair had disengaged itself and fallen loosely over her cheek. She watched Paul, as he began to fall asleep, and stroked his hair . . . for a long time . . . and waited. The rain drummed on the window.

"Call our secret call from where you are," she whispered softly, so as not to waken Paul, who was now asleep, "and I shall call back . . ." And these words she repeated several times, and sighed shiveringly.

The rain drummed and she waited.

VIII

MICHAEL, LONG SINCE having abandoned his tears, was now uproariously drunk. He had overturned his table and the waiters were leading him to the door.

"Revolt! Revolt!" he kept mumbling drunkenly, and even as they were pushing him out into the rain, and the customers were laughing, he kept on repeating these words out loud. He had been forced to pay for the glasses he'd broken, and now, with the change in a crumpled heap in his hand, he waved it at the wind and rain. He started up the boulevard, staggering, and once he almost fell in a puddle. Pedestrians hurrying by in the rain gave him only briefly curious glances.

Michael weaved along the boulevard, and then paused to rest on a bench dripping with rain. There, stuffing the money back into his pockets, he leaned his head in his hands and stared at a puddle at his feet.

"I refuse!" he choked, and got up and walked on.

By now he had reached the bridge and began walking along the concrete ramp. Below, the river, softly needled by the rain, flowed by slowly and in darkness. A tugboat hooted and blew up steam towards the bridge. Michael stopped midway across the bridge and leaned on the railing to look down. He was standing in the shadows, and the rain pattered down all around him.

"It's cold!" he cried, and a gust of wind blew by, driving rain against his face. "It's cold!" he repeated with mounting disgust.

The bridge, at this point, was completely deserted, except for one trolley car that clanged and rattled by. As it passed, Michael opened his mouth and screamed in the midst of the clamor. Then he began to moan and sway, shivering, and huddling up in his coat.

'I've never approved of this method,' he thought. 'It's much too inconvenient, and too cold—But I've made my pact; I've made my pact. I'll show him—the poisoner!' "God has poisoned me!" he suddenly cried out loud. "Do you hear me? God has poisoned me with his damned essence!" No one was around; the bridge was completely deserted, and a strong wing drove slivers of rain across the arc lights. A big ship bawled in the dark distance.

'But before I do this,' Michael thought, 'I should really see *him*—Paul, Paul. Ha ha! I'll hurl curses in his face, the ape. Making a fool of me, stealing my poetry and saying that he'll burn it, laughing at me, abetting Marie's damned teasing, taunting me—the insensitive, stupid, thick-headed ape! The great genius of love and life, yes, I'll show the ape . . .'

Michael had suddenly begun to walk back in the direction from which he had come. He was muttering to himself out loud. "Perhaps I'm mad now, stark raving mad as they say—" He looked around him, eyes gleaming. "When he sees me, he'll be terrified. A lunatic! I'll bang on his window and tell him his hour's up! I'll smother the wretch to death with me! He'll faint when he sees me! Ho ho! That'll be the topper of them all . . ."

Laughing feverishly, Michael hurried on. Suddenly he stopped and leaned again on the railing. 'It's a waste of time,' he thought. 'I shouldn't even warn him. Yes, that's what this is, this running to see him, it's a sort of warning: he doesn't deserve any sympathy of mine. I've none for him or anyone else. Calls me a failure! A failure!' Michael looked down at the waters below, and carefully considered them.

'They'll think it's a dishonor,' he thought, 'but little they'll know—it's not dishonor to be defeated by God. He's put this idea in my head; he wants me out of the way— because I was seeking his impulse: and don't think that I wouldn't have found it, if I had had the fortitude to live on. No doubt about that, I know my powers! But the struggle isn't worth it. Struggle is not happiness. I thought I would find happiness there, curiously enough—It's a good thing I've been warning Arthur. I should really go and see Arthur before I do this, and warn him again, specifically this time. The consequences are what he craves, hey? I'll bet—when the time comes, he won't be so sophomorically secure behind his artistic philosophies, oh no! But maybe he's shrewder than me, that's possible . . . Well, this is all a pretty waste of time.'

Michael suddenly leaned far over the railing until his feet were off the pavement and he was holding himself only by the force of his hands, which were knotted around the bars. "Say something, death," he called to the waters below. "Smug, silent death, omniscient death, sottish death. They tell me corpses dragged out of rivers are bloated, blue, and black, like puffed up bullfrogs, that they glisten with scum, and that the eyes are eaten out by rats . . ." Michael opened and closed his eyes. "That's about to happen to me!" He was so drunk now, that he almost lost his balance; but he only laughed. The darkness below him was swirling dizzily, and he began to feel sick from the Pernod. "Now!" he muttered. "This is how it will feel when I am plunging into the *gouffre!* Just like this! A note, should have written a note! Still time! Oh, it's cold, cold, cold! . . ."

PAUL, ASLEEP IN HELEN'S ARMS, was suddenly awake and shivering all over very violently. Helen's hand, which had been stroking his hair, paused over his head. Paul opened his eyes.

"I'm *cold!*" he pronounced hoarsely. Then, recognizing Helen, he plunged his face into her bosom and shivered violently again, as though he had a chill. "I'm cold, Helen. Is it so cold in the room?"

Helen frowned and placed tender fingertips on his brow.

"No, darling, it's not so cold . . . I don't feel it. But your brow is all wet. You have a fever!"

Paul was shaking in her arms. Helen underwent a spasm of anxiety. "Paul," she cried, "you're sick!" She started to get up.

Paul detained her with his hand. "No, wait," he said. "Now, I feel all right. I'm not cold any more, and look, I'm not shaking any more . . ."

"I don't know—your face is all wet."

"I must have been dreaming," Paul assured her. "What have you been doing, sleeping?"

"I've been watching you, and waiting."

"Do you trust me?"

"I love you and I trust you."

"That's all that counts, then," Paul said, and brought his head back to her bosom. "Oh, it's still raining. What a terrible, terrible night. And all we do is wait and wait . . . Helen, can't I go out and look for him? He's in the bar, Leo told us . . ."

"No," Helen said firmly.

"But I tell you—"

"No. We can't go to him. Don't you know that he has to come to us?"

Paul was silent. "That's nonsense," he finally said.

"Not so much as you think," Helen affirmed. "Let him come to us."

"I can't sleep any more," Paul said. "I think I'll get up and prepare two cups of coffee, and I have some cookies in a bag."

"Let me do it."

"No, no!" cried Paul, jumping up and laughing. "Let me do it. You're my guest. You've just arrived from a long journey, and I'm serving you in my role as a host."

Helen smiled. "Paul, you can be so silly sometimes . . ."

"Now stay right there," Paul cried, running to his cupboard—for that was what he called it, his cupboard—and beginning to rummage around. "I'll bring you the whole meal on a tray, as though you were a queen. And that—" he said, turning triumphantly to Helen—"that is what you are, a queen! My queen!" He ran over and kissed Helen; then he dashed back to his cupboard. "The Queen of the Golden Age. Did you hear that? The Queen of the Golden Age! That's what Michael would call you now, you know. He has all kinds of fancy terms for simple beauty. He would call you a symbol of beauty, perhaps *the* symbol of beauty, in the manner of all the poets and artists! They're all crazy . . ."

Suddenly, a violent knocking came on the window from outside, accompanied by a thick cry.

"What's that?" Paul asked, going towards the window.

Helen didn't answer.

Paul hastened out into the hall and went up to open the outside door. A cold gust of rain blew in. Michael was standing in a puddle, with the rain dripping down his face, glaring madly at Paul.

"Do I look mad?" he cried eagerly.

"Good Lord! You're soaking wet!" cried Paul. "Come on in and dry up."

"No!" thundered Michael. "I asked you, do I look mad?"

"Yes, quite!"

Michael smiled with satisfaction and shook his head to clear it of rain. "Now will you come in?" Paul yelled, for the wind was blowing hard and the rain was making a great splattering noise.

Michael was smiling strangely in the darkness. "I've come to tell you," he said, barely audible in the rainfall, "that this is your last night on earth. It's going to be awful cold, my friend, where you and I are going, the water, and the earth."

A flurry of wind drove by them and Paul cried, "Come on in, you fool!"

"Did you hear what I said? Your last night on earth?"

"I don't care," yelled Paul impatiently, still standing in the doorway.

"I'll bet you're wondering why I'm going to do it," Michael went on, shouting against the rain, even though now he stood right in front of Paul and had his face right next to his. "Don't you want to know the details? The motive, you ape?"

Paul shook his head bewilderedly.

"Oh," Michael said, "so you think that there aren't any specific details to this, hey, no motives? A man commits suicide just because the idea appeals to him, is that it? Well, you're lucky. I wasn't going to come, because I have no sympathy for you, Paul—but something drove me here, some idea. Well, now you're going to listen to me—"

"You're not going to commit suicide," Paul interrupted. He began to smile angelically and blush.

"And why not?" Michael demanded suspiciously.

"Come in and I'll show you why," Paul replied, still smiling.

"No!" yelled Michael again. "Good-bye!" He had moved off towards the stone steps, and Paul had suddenly run out after him and was clutching at his coat.

"Wait a minute!" They were both standing in the rain now, and Paul was soon drenched with rain.

"I wept," said Michael simply, turning his face to Paul's.

"Paul!" he suddenly cried, taking the other's hand and squeezing it. "Paul, a man was killed. All today, after what happened . . . Did you see how Marie treated me? I don't care about her, but I tell you she's an impostor, that one; she revels in evil, she's not a human being!"

"You're being childish."

"Oh, no, I don't think so. There are reasons. I wish I could see Arthur before I do this, and warn him. I was thinking about him on the bridge—it will be on the bridge. Well, Paul—" He began to pull away. But suddenly he went on: "And I was sick in the bar, and they threw me out. Do you know where I'm going to sleep tonight? I'm going to sleep in the river, alone! And you!" he added with savage triumph, "you are going to just expire in your mean little hovel . . ."

"Michael—"

"Do you want some money, Paul? Ha ha ha. Want some money? Here!" Michael drew out a wad of bills from his coat pocket and scattered them like seed, with a broad sweep of his arm, at Paul's feet. "Stoop! And pick them up. They're all yours. Spend them within the next ten minutes, for that's how long you have to live. Ha ha ha!"

Paul was now holding Michael firmly by the arm, and rain poured down both their backs.

"Good-bye," said Michael, straining away from the

other's grip. "This is the way the world ends, you know. Come with me and I'll recite you all the death lyrics in literature, and the love lyrics, too, just to prove to you how far they fall off the mark. I had the mark!—But it was poisoned; it was the forbidden fruit with poison in it! I have a fever, now, I think I'm sick—that's where I'm getting all the courage to do this . . ."

Paul hung on to his arm and said nothing.

"Remember the time I tried to hit you with the floor lamp?" Michael shouted. "Oh, I'm remembering everything now, and all the things I wrote that don't mean anything, and the things I wrote that meant too much. On human terms, you see, that's how life is. On human terms. I don't want those terms. They're ugly; there's no more beauty. I revolt! I refuse! I'm finished! God's defeated me . . ."

Paul smiled grimly.

"You smile? Do you think it's a dishonor to be defeated by God?"

"No," Paul said simply.

"Do you know what it's like?" Michael asked, his eyes gleaming at Paul. "It's like being a fish trying to live on land. One suffocates. I'm suffocating in the ether; God's air is choking me. I went to it in all innocence, I didn't know it would choke me. Now, am I supposed to return to human conditions? Hey? Well, I damned well refuse, that's all. Let me go, damn you, let me go!" And with this, Michael wrenched away violently. But, no sooner having done this, he himself grasped Paul's arm. "Now," he said, "Prometheus—that's a funny one, Prometheus: Arthur called me that this afternoon—well, now, Prometheus bids thee farewell . . ."

Michael interrupted himself with a violent cough. "I'm sick," he choked. "I'm too sick to live. *Dégout! Dégout!* I abandon all my natural rights . . ." He went on talking thickly, and Paul no longer could make out what he was saying; and suddenly Michael's face lit up. "Paul!" he cried. "I just remembered. You have my poetry with you, in your room. I want it! I want it to go down with me!"

"Certainly!" cried Paul happily. "Go in and get it!"

"Are you hinting anything?" yelled Michael suspiciously. "Get out of my way—I'm going to get it!" And with this he lunged past Paul, almost knocking him down, and lumbered heavily into the hall. Paul was right at his heels.

"It's got to go with me, as a symbol of my failure," Michael was muttering. He went into Paul's room and wavered uncertainly. "Where is it?" he demanded menacingly.

Paul was in the doorway. "On my desk," he said. "There."

Michael scuffled to the desk and scooped up the papers,

and folded them in a heap to fit into his coat pocket. Turning, he saw Helen standing by the couch in a shadowy corner of the room. He rubbed his hand across his jaw, and smiled inwardly.

"I'm having visions," he told Paul. Staggering, he walked towards the door. "Visions! It's wonderful. I just saw her . . ."

"Well?" Paul drawled, still standing in the doorway and blocking the way.

"Out of my way," said Michael, waving his heap of papers.

"It isn't a vision," said Paul quietly. "She is here. I told you she would come."

Michael frowned at Paul, and his lips began to tremble. He turned awkwardly, almost fearfully, and looked once again towards the shadowy corner. Helen came out of the shadows and walked soundlessly to Michael and Paul. The papers dropped out of Michael's hand and he breathed out the name, as though he didn't believe what he saw, and was afraid to believe. His clothes were dripping wet, and a little pool was forming at his feet; rain water poured down from his face, and now he was as pale as a sheet.

Helen stopped just three feet away and gazed anxiously at Michael, a small wrinkle forming on her smooth white brow. One hand, she partly held out, trembling faintly . . .

Michael's eyes opened wide with some sort of terror. He was trying to mumble something, his lips were working. Finally, he managed to mutter out, in a hoarse whisper, "I . . . thought . . . I . . . had no right . . . to . . . ever . . . see . . . you . . . again."

Helen advanced another foot.

"Why not?" she asked clearly.

Paul, standing in the doorway, was feeling so faint he didn't dare speak; he thrust his hands in his pockets, because they were trembling; and leaned against the door-jamb in an attitude of complete exhaustion, watching Michael with something of fearful expectation. He opened his mouth to say, "Michael," but no sound issued from his throat.

"Because . . ." Michael was whispering awesomely, his eyes fastened on Helen's face, " . . . because . . . of what . . . I've . . . done."

"What have you done?" Helen demanded softly.

Michael was swaying on his feet. "Lived?" he whispered.

"That's probably all," Helen said. "Don't you think you're good enough for me?" She was almost on the verge of tears.

Michael sobbed out one word, "No," in a great quivering cry, and fell to his knees before Helen, and lay there huddled and weeping pathetically. Helen, with a groan of despair, immediately knelt down on the floor beside him and took him into her arms.

Slowly, Paul closed the door and wavered across the room to sit on the couch and watch. There he sat.

Michael was almost hysterical; his weeping grew more and more profuse. Helen said nothing, but only leaned her head against his and closed her eyes; and cupping Michael's face in her hands, she rocked his head gently back and forth, as though to lull away his tears . . .

Paul sat for a long while watching. Suddenly, he realized that the rain had stopped; there was only the sound of dripping eaves, and of a gentle breeze. He rose from the couch and went over to the window to open it.

Michael was holding the weight of Helen's dark hair in the palm of his hand and awesomely looking at it.

Now—explosively, for there had been much silence— Paul said, "Well! So one rejoins his true love and the occasion is all tears! That's the so-called poet all over. And money lying outside in the street!" Paul went to the door. He stopped and gazed down at the two on the floor. Then, since they were both smiling up at him, he kneeled in front of them and took both their hands, while they too clasped hands. "The fault," Paul said to Michael, "is with you, and not with anything else, not even God . . . If you actually know how to love her—though she can be bitter—she can flood your soul with light, all of your soul! Aren't I right? Helen, tell him—I'm right!"

Helen pressed both their hands tightly and only smiled . . .

And in this manner, amid the happy endearments of the woman, and the silence of thought and imagination, the miracle of wholeness was renewed.

AT MIDNIGHT, LEO, his studies finished, put out the light in his room and went down the dormitory hall. He knocked at Arthur's door.

"Come in!"

Arthur was seated at his desk, writing.

"What are you doing?"

"Writing some poetry."

"What about examinations?"

"Tomorrow."

Leo sat on the edge of Arthur's desk. "I came here earlier," he said, "but you weren't in. I wanted to tell you something amazing: I went to Paul's tonight, and there, with him in his dirty little room, was the most beautiful girl I ever saw in my life, and her name was Helen."

"Helen?" Arthur exclaimed. "Why, that's the name Paul used to get Michael so mad the night of the party."

"Yes."

"Do you think they're still there?"

"I guess so, but Paul wouldn't let me in. He closed the door in my face."

"Let's go there," Arthur said, rising and putting on his coat. "And where's Michael?"

"I left him in the Boulevard Bar. He was weeping and getting drunk."

"Good Lord!"

They started down the stairs. Arthur seemed very excited: "I was just working out something," he told Leo happily. "I want to show it to Michael."

"What is it?"

"It isn't finished yet. It's an idea. A poem about the poet and God."

They were out on the street; it had stopped raining. Great gaps in the clouds revealed clusters of stars, and over across the sodden campus darkness, the boulevard glistened in the freshness and glitter of the lights.

Julius was just then coming across the campus and they met him.

"I've just been to the Boulevard Bar," he said. "They told me that Michael was thrown out for disturbing the peace, upsetting the table."

"Oh my God!" cried Leo, laughing. "I should have taken him home. I knew he'd get too drunk!"

"Come on with us," Arthur told Julius. "We're going over to Paul's to see the mysterious Helen we've heard so much about."

"Helen?" exclaimed Julius, suddenly quite interested.

"Yes. And Leo claims her to be the most beautiful girl he ever saw."

They hastened down M street and turned to enter Paul's gate.

"There's no light," put in Leo.

Arthur pushed open the hall door and they all trooped in; in Paul's room, they lit a match and found an oil lamp. There was no one there, and even the old tattered raincoat that had hung on a nail for months besides the little table was gone. Just a pair of old shoes beneath the bed.

"Let's go see if they're in the Boulevard Bar," Arthur suggested. "They must be around somewhere."

"It's strange," Julius said softly.

"Why?"

"I don't know."

Once again in the street, they marched three abreast towards the bar. Suddenly, Leo cried out and pointed up the boulevard.

"There! There's Paul now, and he's with *her!*"

Arthur and Julius turned to see.

"But you're crazy," Julius said. "That's not Paul. That's Michael."

"It's Paul's old raincoat . . . don't you recognize him? Let's catch up to them." And they started hurrying up the boulevard.

Helen and her lover were standing on a trolley island in the middle of the boulevard, just beneath a street lamp, with arms entwined around each other's waists. A trolley was clanging towards them.

"But he's too tall to be Paul," Julius was saying as he hurried along after Arthur and Leo. "Michael's taller."

"Nonsense," laughed Leo. "He's too husky to be Michael."

"Hey!" Arthur now yelled, as he hastened his footsteps and waved his hand at Helen and her lover. Helen turned and smiled. To Leo and Julius, Arthur said: "She does look beautiful from here, that Helen. I've always wanted to meet her, after all the mystery that enshrouded her! . . ."

The trolley was now pulling up in front of the two people on the island and stopping. Helen turned once again and waved her hand at the oncoming students.

"There," Arthur said, hurrying. "She's waving at us. But look! They look as though . . . They are! They're getting into the trolley!"

"Well!" snapped Julius, a little peeved. "There's no sense in hurrying any further." He stopped in his tracks. They were still about a hundred or so feet from the trolley island. Helen and the others had gotten into the trolley and now it was pulling away and clanging its bell.

"Well!" panted Arthur, a bit disappointed, with arms akimbo, standing and watching the departing trolley.

Then they saw Michael, or Paul, or whomever they thought it was, come to the back window of the trolley and wave at them as it reeled away. Helen was at his side, and she, too, was waving.

Then, in another moment, the trolley was on the bridge and speeding over the river towards the outskirts of the city.

"They should at least have waited for us," Leo was now saying sadly. "But I guess they wanted to catch that trolley. Damn that Paul."

"It wasn't Paul!" Julius insisted again.

"Well, whoever it was," Leo went on disconsolately, "I have a feeling we'll never see them again, neither one of them. I can feel it by the way they were waving us good-bye."

"Don't be silly," said Arthur. "Well, we might as well go to the Boulevard Bar and have a few drinks. I want to show you my poetry."

"It was Michael," Julius was still insisting to Leo.

Leo sighed and waved an impatient hand at him. "All right, all right. But we'll never see them again."

They were all three very silent as they walked to the Boulevard Bar. And of course, they were indeed destined never to see Paul or Michael again—as Leo had instinctively divined—but they were not destined to form any vague notion of what had really happened that night until several weeks later, when Arthur, coming back from a class one day, found a letter in his mailbox.

It read: "Amenehmet looks upon the beauty of the sun!"—a quotation which Arthur remembered from his studies in Egyptian history—and it was signed, "Orpheus." This was when the first faint understanding of the full significance of what had happened began to come to Arthur.

EXCERPTS FROM
JACK KEROUAC'S JOURNALS

JOURNALS 1943-'44: JAN. 1944

We are all too sensitive to go on: it is too cold, and our bodies are too exhausted. There is too much life around. The multitude is feverish and ill. There is war where men sleep on the snow, and when we waken from sleep we do not desire to go on. I hiccup very violently, twice. This is an age that has created sick men, all weaklings like me. What we need is a journey to new lands. I shall embark soon on one of these. I shall sleep on the grass and eat fruit for breakfast. Perhaps when I return, I shall be well again.

BRIEF NOTES ON "THE HALF JEST" (*ORPHEUS EMERGED*)

Michael – the genius of imagination and art, 22
Paul – the genius of life and love, 22
Maureen – Michael's mistress, 32 years old
Claude [Arthur] – Michael's friend, a student, 20
Leo – a student, 18
Anthony – Paul's friend, a drunkard and artist, 38

"Toni" – Claude's [Arthur's] girl, 21
Jules – a strange student, 17
Marie – Dmitri's [Anthony's] beautiful wife, 27
"Barbara" – Maureen's friend, 25
"Robert"– a psychopath, 26
Helen – the beloved of Marcel Opheus, 21
Marcel Orpheus, who is never seen, 22
Setting – A large city called West, in the land of Promethea
– or vice versa.

M. has suffered the wound of his calling and deliberately
sold out P. The story concerns P.'s return and the ultimate
rejoining, and the struggle with appropriate principles
involved.

JOURNALS 1943-'44
PLOT STRUCTURE OF NOVELETTE

I. Paul in bookstore; on way to class with Leo, pathetically expresses his desire for learning; class scene, Claude
[Arthur] introduced; then to Paul's cellar room; Dmitri
[Anthony] there with problem; poverty and few pathetic
books, and picture of Helen.

II. Paul's call on Michael; patches up things for Dmitri
[Anthony]; Marie's ennui emphasized; a call from Michael;
she half-heartedly repels him; his offer; meets Dmitri
[Anthony] coming in

III. Party scene, where Paul's mention of Helen and Michael's rage, Michael's growing desire for Marie, are shown, etc. etc.

IV. A week later. Paul has been away "sleeping in grass and eating fruit for breakfast." He returns—it is a cloudy, ominous day—he meets Leo in park, they call on Michael. Maureen tells them that M. has been gone several days on a trip. P. picks up some of M.'s poetry and mockingly reads it to Leo. They meet Claude [Arthur], who tells them that M. and Marie have been living together in Bohemian Quarter. At this, Paul rushes to Dmitri's [Anthony's], where Marie has already returned. Dmitri [Anthony] is a wreck; Marie ministers him. Michael and Claude [Arthur] arrive; scene between M. and Marie. It begins to rain. M. goes to bar, Paul to his hovel—he feels he must, there he finds Helen waiting, etc.

Symbolized Idea—M. trying to transcend human emotions to those of God—emotions of creation, or of Eternity, etc. Thus he abandons his human self, Paul, and strikes off for the High Regions. But there he finds himself lost, lonely, and out of his element: his species-self, biologically speaking, holds him back. A fish trying to live out of water, on air alone, M. finds that his life exists unquestionably on human terms: he cannot be God, or be like him, because he is human. This makes him see that the highest state he can attain is that of the "Lyre of God," and in a contemporaneous sense, that of God's representative to man. "A high meeting . . ." As Orpheus, the artist-man, rather than merely man, or merely Prometheus (the artist), he achieves his great goal of wholeness. *This* is a "new vision"—possible only after the cold windy darknesses of the High Regions have been explored. The "Impulse of God" poem key to M.'s whole *success*—but he transcends, yet maintains, this success to that of *wholeness plus vision.*

BOOK OF SYMBOLS 1944

The modern artist must discover new forms or he will perish by the hand of action.

—Narrative
   —Poetic prose
   —Facts
   Time Factor – 3 prongs
   (1) Sunset at six – Saroyan period (in Hartford)
   (2) Galloway – Joycean period
   (3) The Haunted Life – Wolfean period
   (4) I Bid You Lose Me – Nietzschean period (Neo-Rimbaudian)
   (5) Orpheus Emerged – post-Nietzschean period (Yeats period)
   (6) Phillip Tourian Novel – Spenglerian period

(2½) The Sea is My Brother – American period (Dos Passos)

(3½) Supreme Reality – post-neurotic period

Dos Passos's new form (U.S.A.) severely misused. A truly creative artist hampered by excessive naturalism.

On this page, you see, I take up the thread of my creative life and play with it awhile. I don't live by the calendar of personal events, but by the almanac of artistic directions.

January 1945 – Edie all right. Returned to N.Y. to try and make good so we can live together in N.Y. Wrote essay, story, poem—all determined by new ideas. Cont'd work on novel with Burroughs.

Feb. – Complete novel with Burroughs. Crucial sense of "end" and "beginning." Also completed essay on Nietzsche, Blake, and Yeats; short novel, "Orpheus Emerged"; story, "God's Daughter."

March – Seeing a lot of Burroughs. He is responsible for the education of Lucien, whom I had found, in lieu of his anarchy (rather than in spite of it), an extremely important person. "I lean with fearful attraction over the depths of each creature's possibilities and weep for all that lies atrophied under the heavy lid of custom and morality"—and—"The bastard alone has the right to be natural." (Gide) These lines elicit a picture of the Burroughs thought. However, the psychoanalytical probing has upset me prodigiously.

THE BEAT MOVEMENT

In the 1950s, a group of writers and artists began to respond to a growing sense of alienation and psychic emptiness in postwar America. They felt the culture was restrictive, hypocritical, repressed, and they were especially appalled by the virulent racism that continued to poison the soul of the country. Their general idea was to open things up. They derived their energy from an expansive belief in the American traditions of freedom and adventure, of infinite invention and possibility. They found spiritual renewal through a connection with submerged black culture. They sought to break free from the Puritan denial of sex and presaged the "sexual revolution" by freely expressing desire and openly extolling pleasure. Their message to a generation that felt boxed-in, shut-down, and spiritually lost: Get out onto the open road and rediscover your lost American freedom.

The phrase "beat generation" came out of a specific conversation between Jack Kerouac and John Clellon Holmes in 1948 in which Kerouac distinguished his generation from the glamorous Lost Generation. Kerouac most likely picked up the word "beat" from his friend Herbert Huncke, who was familiar with the street lingo of the time. "Beat" connoted broke, homeless, exhausted, emptied out. But Kerouac also used the word to imply "beatific." Holmes wrote an article for *The New York Times Magazine* in 1952 which was headlined, "This Is the Beat Generation," and when Kerouac later published an excerpt from *On the Road* called "Jazz of the Beat Generation," the term took hold.

The main figures in the movement were situated in New York and California. New York City writers associated with the Beats include Jack Kerouac, Neal Cassady, Holmes, Allen Ginsberg, Gregory Corso, Huncke, Le Roi Jones, Diane DiPrima, and William Burroughs; in San Francisco were Gary Snyder, Lawrence Ferlinghetti, Kenneth Rexroth, Philip Whalen, Robert Creeley, and Michael McClure. A number of these writers (including Kerouac, Whalen, Snyder, and Ginsberg) became involved in meditation and Buddhism. City Lights Books, established in San Francisco by Ferlinghetti, was a key factor, both as a bookshop and publisher, in making the work of the Beats known. The quintessential texts of the movement are Ginsberg's *Howl*, Kerouac's *On the Road*, and Burroughs' *Naked Lunch*.

But the Beat Movement was more than the output of these poets and writers. The Beat sensibility was shared by painters (Larry Rivers), filmmakers and photographers (Robert Frank and Alfred Leslie), musicians (David Amram), and others who considered themselves connected to the long tradition of bohemianism in America.

As is often the case with counter-cultural, anti-establishment, outsider movements, the mainstream culture eventually found ways to categorize, caricature, de-value, and ultimately co-opt the Beats. They were depicted in the media as crazy beret-wearing and bongo-beating weirdos, conspiratorial commies, amoral homos, filthy drug-addicted hipsters, or just no-talent losers and hangers-on. The media frenzy actually turned the Beat Movement into a fad, and inevitably the established literary and art-criticism world did not take the work seriously.

Over time, however, the works generated by the Beats have emerged as lasting, valuable contributions to the culture, and the ideas informing those works have endured. In an article published in 1982, Ginsberg characterized some of the effects of the Beat ethos in these terms:

Spiritual liberation, sexual "revolution" or "liberation," i.e., gay liberation, somewhat catalyzing women's liberation, black liberation, Gray Panther activism.

Liberation of the word from censorship.

Demystification and/or decriminalization of some laws against marijuana and other drugs.

The evolution of rhythm and blues into rock and roll as a high art form, as evidenced by the Beatles, Bob Dylan, and other popular musicians influenced in the late fifties and sixties by Beat generation poets' and writers' works.

The spread of ecological consciousness, emphasized early on by Gary Snyder and Michael McClure's notion of a "Fresh Planet."

Opposition to the military-industrial machine civilization, as emphasized in the writings of Burroughs, Huncke, Ginsberg, and Kerouac.

Attention to what Kerouac called (after Spengler) a "second religiousness" developing within an advanced civilization.

Return to an appreciation of idiosyncrasy as against state regimentation.

Respect for land and indigenous peoples and creatures, as proclaimed by Kerouac in his slogan from *On the Road*: "The Earth is an Indian thing."

The Beats are now generally regarded as the venerable upholders of the great American traditions that were set forth by Thoreau and Whitman. Their attitude, style, and approach to life first resonated in the youth of the postwar period. But their spirit and their ideas—pacifism, reverence for nature and naturalness, consciousness-enhancement/expansion, faith in the divinity of the self—and the art they created will continue to influence and inspire young people of all generations.

BRIEF BIOGRAPHY

Jack Kerouac was born in working-class Lowell, Massachusetts, in 1922, the youngest of three children in a Franco-American family. He spoke a dialect of French before he learned English. His older brother Gerard died of rheumatic fever at the age of nine.

He attended local Catholic and public schools and won a football scholarship to Columbia University in New York City in 1939. After dropping out of college in the fall of 1941, he tried unsuccessfully to fit in with the military, worked as a deck hand in the Merchant Marine, and returned to New York, where he met Columbia students Allen Ginsberg and Lucien Carr, their strange downtown friend William Burroughs, and the joyful street cowboy from Denver named Neal Cassady.

His first novel, *The Town and the City*, an account of his youth in Lowell and New York City, appeared in 1950, and was well received. But it was not until the publication of *On the Road* that he became the rebel/cult hero who epitomized the style of living and writing associated with the Beat movement. Narrated by Sal Paradise (Kerouac), *On the*

Road is a picaresque chronicle of hitchhiking trips across America with Dean Moriarty (Neal Cassady), Carlo Marx (Ginsberg), and others. The novel was originally written as one paragraph on a long roll of paper. Only after six years of revision and rejection did it find a publisher, but when *On the Road* finally appeared, Kerouac's place as one of the best-known and controversial writers of his time was secured. With his confessional approach, long stream-of-consciousness sentences and page-long paragraphs, he revolutionized American prose.

During the period before *On the Road* came out, Kerouac crisscrossed the country, following Ginsberg and Cassady to California, where he befriended the Zen poet Gary Snyder, and embraced Buddhism. But the phenomenal success of *On the Road* made Kerouac an icon. In the long run, he did not thrive in the spotlight, and literary critics, dismayed by the "Beatnik fad," refused to take Kerouac seriously as a writer.

Publication of his many other books followed, among them the novels *The Dharma Bums*, *The Subterraneans*, and *Big Sur*, as well a several volumes of poetry and other writings. Kerouac considered all of his "true story novels" to be parts of one vast book, the story of his lifetime. The Duluoz Legend consists, in chronological order, of *Visions of Gerard*, *Doctor Sax*, *Maggy Cassidy*, *Vanity of Duluoz*, *On the Road*, *Visions of Cody*, *The Subterraneans*, *Tristessa*, *Lone-*

some Traveler, Desolation Angels, The Dharma Bums, Book of Dreams, Big Sur, and *Satori in Paris.*

Kerouac's fictional alter ego, Jack Duluoz, is an alienated, restless, passionate seeker of dharma (the Zen concept of "truth") through new experiences, human adventuring—and drugs, sex, and music along the way.

Toward the end of his life Kerouac, suffering from his celebrity status and relentless critical beating, drank heavily. In 1961 he tried to break his drinking habit and reconnect with his creative spirit by attempting a solitary retreat in a mid-coastal California cabin, a painful effort chronicled in *Big Sur.*

Kerouac married Stella Sampas, a childhood friend with whom he had stayed in touch over the years. Kerouac, Stella, and Jack's mother Gabrielle lived together until Jack's death at the age of 47 in St. Petersburg, Florida, in 1969.

AUTOBIOGRAPHY

(KEROUAC'S INTRODUCTION TO *LONESOME TRAVELER*)

NAME: Jack Kerouac

NATIONALITY: Franco-American

PLACE OF BIRTH: Lowell, Massachusetts

DATE OF BIRTH: March 12, 1922

EDUCATION (schools attended, special courses of study, degrees and years)

Lowell (Mass.) High School; Horace Mann School for Boys; Columbia College (1940-42); New School for Social Research (1948-49). Liberal arts, no degrees (1936–1949). Got an A from Mark Van Doren in English at Columbia (Shakespeare course).—Flunked chemistry at Columbia.— Had a 92 average at Horace Mann School (1939–40). Played football on varsities. Also track, baseball, chess teams. . . .

ORPHEUS EMERGED

SUMMARY OF PRINCIPAL OCCCUPATIONS AND/OR JOBS

Everything: Let's elucidate: scullion on ships, gas station attendant, deckhand on ships, newspaper sportswriter (Lowell Sun), railroad brakeman, script synopsizer for 20th Century Fox in N.Y., soda jerk, railroad yardclerk, also railroad baggagehandler, cottonpicker, assistant furniture mover, sheet metal apprentice on the Pentagon in 1942, forest service fire lookout 1956, construction laborer (1941).

INTERESTS

HOBBIES I invented my own baseball game, on cards, extremely complicated, and am in the process of playing a whole 154-game season among eight clubs, with all the works, batting averages, E.R.A. averages, etc.

SPORTS Played all of them except tennis and lacrosse and skull.

SPECIAL Girls

PLEASE GIVE A BRIEF RESUME OF YOUR LIFE

Had beautiful childhood, my father a printer in Lowell, Mass., roamed fields and riverbanks day and night, wrote little novels in my room, first novel written at age 11, also kept extensive diaries and "newspapers" covering my own-invented horse-racing and baseball and football worlds (as recorded in novel *Doctor Sax*). —Had good early education from Jesuit brothers at St. Joseph's Parochial School in Lowell making me jump sixth grade in public school later on; as child traveled to Montreal, Quebec, with family; was given a horse at age 11 by mayor of Lawrence (Mass.), Billy White, gave rides to all kids in neighborhood; horse ran away. Took long walks under old trees of New England at night with my mother and aunt. Listened to their gossip attentively. Decided to become a writer at age 17 under influence of Sebastian Sampas, local young poet who later died on Anzio beach head; read the life of Jack London at age 18 and decided to also be an adventurer, a lonesome traveler; early literary influences Saroyan and Hemingway; later Wolfe (after I had broken leg in Freshman football at Columbia read Tom [Thomas] Wolfe and roamed his New York on crutches). –Influenced by older brother Gerard Kerouac who died at age 9 in 1925 when I was 4, was great painter and drawer in childhood (he was)—(also said to be a saint by the nuns)—(recorded in novel *Visions of Gerard*).—My father was completely honest man full of gaiety; soured in last years over Roosevelt and World War II and died of cancer of the spleen. –Mother still living, I live with her a kind of monastic life that has enabled me to write as much as I did.—But also wrote on the road, as hobo, railroader, Mexican exile, Europe travel . . . One sister, Caroline, now married to Paul E. Blake Jr. of Henderson N.C., a government antimissile technician—she has one son, Paul Jr., my nephew, who calls me Uncle Jack and loves me.—My mother's name Gabrielle, learned all about natural storytelling from her long stories about Montreal and New Hampshire.—My people go back to Breton France, first North American ancestor Baron Alexandre Louis Lebris de Kerouac of Cornwall, Brittany, 1750 or so, was granted land along the Riviere du Loup after victory of Wolfe over Montcalm; his descendents married Indians (Mohawk and Caughnawaga) and became potato farmers; first United States descendant my grandfather Jean-Baptiste Kerouac, carpenter, Nashua N.H.—My father's mother a Bernier related to explorer Bernier—all Bretons on father's side— My mother has a Norman name, L'Evesque.—

First formal novel *The Town and the City* written in tradition of long work and revision, from 1946 to 1948, three years, published by Harcourt Brace in 1950.—Then discovered "spontaneous" prose and wrote, say *The Subterraneans* in 3 nights—wrote *On the Road* in 3 weeks—

Read and studied alone all my life.—Set a record at Columbia College cutting classes in order to stay in dormitory room to write a daily play and read, say, Louis Ferdinand Celine, instead of "classics" of the course.—

Had own mind.—Am known as "madman bum and angel" with "naked endless head" of "prose."—Also a verse poet, *Mexico City Blues* (Grove, 1959).—Always considered writing my duty on earth. Also the preachment of universal kindness, which hysterical critics have failed to notice beneath frenetic activity of my true-story novels about the "beat" generation.—Am actually not "beat" but strange solitary crazy Catholic mystic . . .

Final plans: hermitage in the woods, quiet writing of old age, mellow hopes of Paradise (which comes to everybody anyway). . . .

© Jack Kerouac, 1960

SELECTED BIBLIOGRAPHY OF BOOKS ABOUT JACK KEROUAC

Amburn, Ellis. *Subterranean Kerouac: The Hidden Life of Jack Kerouac*. New York: St. Martin's Press, 1998.

Cassady, Carolyn. *Heart Beat: My Life with Jack and Neal*. Berkeley: Creative Arts Book Company, 1976.

Cassay, Carolyn. *Off the Road: My Years with Cassady, Kerouac, and Ginsberg*. New York: Penguin, 1991.

Charters, Ann. *Kerouac: A Biography*. San Francisco: Straight Arrow, 1973.

Charters, Ann. *Kerouac: A Biography*. New York: St. Martin's Press, 1994.

Clark, Tom. *Jack Kerouac*. New York: Paragon House, 1984.

Gifford, Barry and Lawrence Lee. *Jack's Book: An Oral Biography of Jack Kerouac*. New York: St. Martin's Press, 1978.

Jarvis, Charles E. *Visions of Kerouac*. Lowell, MA: Ithaca Press, 1974.

Johnson, Joyce. *Minor Characters: A Young Woman's Coming of Age in the Beat Orbit of Jack Kerouac*. New York: Penguin, 1999.

Johnson, Joyce and Jack Kerouac. *Door Wide Open: A Beat Love Affair in Letters, 1957-1958*. New York: Viking Press, 2000.

Jones, James T. *Jack Kerouac's Duluoz Legend: The Mythic Form of an Autobiographical Fiction*. Southern Illinois Press, 1999.

Kazin, Alfred. *Contemporaries*. Boston: Little Brown, 1962.

McDarrah, Fred. *Kerouac and Friends: A Beat Generation Album*. New York: Morrow, 1984.

McNally, Dennis. *Desolation Angel: Jack Kerouac, The Beats and America*. New York: Random House, 1979.

Miles, Barry. *Jack Kerouac King of the Beats: A Portrait*. New York: Henry Holt, 1998.

Sandison, David and Carolyn Cassady. *Jack Kerouac: An Illustrated Biography*. Chicago: Chicago Review Press, 1999.

SELECTED BIBLIOGRAPHY OF BOOKS ABOUT THE BEATS

Ash, Mel. *Beat Spirit: The Way of the Beat Writers as Living Experience*. New York: Putnam, 1997.

The Beat Book. Boston: Shambhala, 1995.

Carr. R. B. Case and F. Dellar. *The Hip: Hipsters, Jazz and the Beat Generation*. Faber and Faber, 1986.

Charters, Anne, editor. *The Portable Beat Reader*. New York: Viking Press, 1992.

Cook, Bruce. *The Beat Generation*. New York: Scribner, 1971.

Duberman, Martin. *Black Mountain: An Exploration in Community*. New York: Dutton Press, 1972.

George-Warren, Holly, editor. *The Rolling Stone Book of the Beats: The Beat Generation and American Culture*. New York: Hyperion, 1999.

Gold, Herbert. *Bohemia: Digging the Roots of Cool*. New York: Simon & Schuster/Touchstone, 1994.

Gruen, John, photographs by Fred McDarrah. *The New Bohemia*. Chicago: A Cappella, 1990.

Halberstam, David. *The Fifties*. New York: Villard Books, 1993.

Mailer, Norman. *The White Negro*. San Francisco: City Lights, 1957.

McClure, Michael. *Scratching the Beat Surface*. North Point, 1992.

McDarrah, Fred and Gloria. *The Beat Generation: Glory Days in Greenwich Village*. Schirmer Books, 1996.

Miles, Barry. *The Beat Hotel: Ginsberg, Burroughs, and Corso in Paris, 1958-1963*. New York: Grove Press, 2000.

Morgan, Bill. *The Beat Generation in New York: A Walking Tour of Jack Kerouac's City*. San Fransisco: City Lights, 1997.

Tytell, John. *Naked Angels: The Life and Literature of the Beat Generation*. New York: McGraw-Hill, 1976.

Tytell, John, photographs by Mellon. *Paradise Outlaws: Remembering the Beats*. New York: William Morrow, 1999.

Waldman, Anne, editor. *The Beat Book: Writings from the Beat Generation*.